NATSUME SŌSEKI is universally recognized to be Japan's greatest modern novelist. Born Natsume Kinnosuke in Edo in 1867, the year before the city was renamed Tokyo, he survived a lonely childhood, being traded between foster and biological parents, was deeply schooled in both the Chinese classics and English, and at the age of twenty-two chose from a Chinese source the defiantly playful pen name Sōseki ('Garglestone') to signify his sense of his own eccentricity. In 1893, Sōseki became the second graduate of (Tokyo) Imperial University's English Department and entered the graduate program, but in 1895 he abruptly took a position teaching English in a rural middle school. Though hoping to become a writer as early as the age of fourteen, Sōseki chose the more respectable path of English literature scholar, was sent to London by the Ministry of Education in 1900 for two years, and taught in his alma mater until 1907, when his early success as a part-time writer of stories and novels led him to accept a position as staff novelist for the *Asahi Shinbun* newspaper, in which he serialized the rest of his fourteen novels. Sōseki also published substantial works of literary theory and history (and contemplative essays, memoirs, lectures on the individual and society, etc.) and continued to think of himself as a scholar after his controversial resignation from the university. His works quickly lost any hint of academic artifice, however, relying initially on a freewheeling sense of humor, and then darkening as Sōseki wrestled with increasingly debilitating bouts of depression and illness. Sōseki wrote many Chinese poems and haiku as a form of escape from the stresses of the world he had created. He died in 1916 with his last – and longest – novel still unfinished. Each new generation of Japanese readers rediscovers Sōseki, and Western readers find in him a truly original voice among those artists who have most fully grasped the human experience.

J. COHN studied Japanese at Cornell and Harvard universities, as well as in Japan, and has taught Japanese literature at Harvard University and the University of Hawaii. He is the author of a study on the comic spirit in modern Japanese fiction.

NATSUME SŌSEKI

Botchan

Translated and introduced by
J. COHN

PENGUIN BOOKS

PENGUIN CLASSICS

Published by the Penguin Group
Penguin Books Ltd, 80 Strand, London WC2R ORL, England
Penguin Group (USA) Inc., 375 Hudson Street, New York, New York 10014, USA
Penguin Group (Canada), 90 Eglinton Avenue East, Suite 700, Toronto, Ontario, Canada M4P 2Y3
(a division of Pearson Penguin Canada Inc.)
Penguin Ireland, 25 St Stephen's Green, Dublin 2, Ireland (a division of Penguin Books Ltd)
Penguin Group (Australia), 707 Collins Street, Melbourne, Victoria 3008, Australia
(a division of Pearson Australia Group Pty Ltd)
Penguin Books India Pvt Ltd, 11 Community Centre, Panchsheel Park, New Delhi – 110 017, India
Penguin Group (NZ), 67 Apollo Drive, Rosedale, Auckland 0632, New Zealand
(a division of Pearson New Zealand Ltd)
Penguin Books (South Africa) (Pty) Ltd, Block D, Rosebank Office Park, 181 Jan Smuts Avenue,
Parktown North, Gauteng 2193, South Africa

Penguin Books Ltd, Registered Offices: 80 Strand, London WC2R ORL, England

www.penguin.com

First published in Japanese in 1906
This translation first published in Japan by Kodansha International Ltd. 2005
This edition first published in Penguin Classics 2012

021

Translation copyright © Joel Cohn, 2005
Chronology copyright © Jay Rubin, 2009
All rights reserved

The moral right of the translator and the author of the chronology has been asserted

Set in Sabon 10.25/12.25 pt
Typeset by Palimpsest Book Production Limited, Falkirk, Stirlingshire
Printed and bound in Great Britain by Clays Ltd, Elcograf S.p.A.

ISBN: 978-0-141-39188-5

www.greenpenguin.co.uk

Contents

Introduction

Botchan takes its title from the nickname given to the main character, who doubles as the novel's narrator, by the devoted old family maidservant Kiyo. Applied exclusively to boys and young men of respectable families, along with the occasional adult male who has not quite managed to grow up, the term can be used either as a description or as one of the many titles that are called upon to serve as a substitute for personal names in Japan. It may be used to express a measure of respect mixed with fondness for and intimacy with its subject, as Kiyo does; at other times it carries a mildly dismissive tone. It has several connotations, sometimes conceived of as interrelated and sometimes taken as independent of each other: a younger son; inexperienced or naive; easygoing in a way that can either be mildly endearing or distressingly irresponsible; or, in extreme cases, spoiled rotten. All of these, except for the last, apply to the title character to a greater or lesser degree, but there is more to him than the sum of these parts, and some of his qualities are quite the opposite of what the term might lead us to expect.

A century on from its initial publication, *Botchan* remains one of the most familiar, most read, and most loved of all novels in Japan. Its popularity has persisted even as the Japan it depicts, where a crash program of modernization was transforming every aspect of life but the ways of the feudal period still remained a living memory, has itself passed into the realm of distant nostalgia. It has also managed to survive its adoption as a school text, a fate that might well have proved to be a kiss of

death for a less appealing book. Yet for all its obvious merits –
among them its tangy style, refreshingly lighthearted yet
tough-minded spirit, sparkling humor, and an array of colorful
characters known by memorable nicknames – there is still
something a little odd, a little idiosyncratic about this enduring
popularity.

Artistically it is not an especially polished work: its phrasing
and structure are often loose and bumpy, not surprisingly for a
novel dashed off by a young professor of English who seems to
have been more intent on venting his frustrations and amusing
a small audience of associates than on reaching for immortality.
It offers few hints of the psychological and philosophical depth
that distinguish Natsume Sōseki's later novels (which were soon
to establish him as Japan's pre-eminent modern novelist, a position from which he has never fallen), or of the exquisite
suggestiveness, penetrating insights, or inventive brilliance of so
many later Japanese writers. While Botchan's upright, straight-
forward nature is occasionally cited as an embodiment of
'typical' Japanese character, surely it is significant that Sōseki
portrays him and the few kindred spirits he finds as the exceptions in a society dominated by hypocrites and schemers.

This, in fact, may be a key to its popularity: if anything, what
is atypical about it, the way that it differs from so many other
classics, may be precisely what has continued to appeal to
generations of Japanese readers even as their world has continued to change, sometimes drastically, all around them. The voice
in which Botchan tells his story is striking, not quite like anything
seen in Japanese fiction before, and not often matched since:
sometimes choppy but always vivid, direct, and outspoken; basically colloquial but frequently enriched by literary expressions
at strategic points. The reader has the sense of being in direct
touch with an engaging, refreshingly candid character who may
do some boasting but never talks down to us. The contrast
between his forthrightness and the devious, pompous tones of
many of the other characters makes him all the more appealing.

Botchan's language is a superb fit for what must be the principal attraction of the novel for many readers – its irreverent,
accept-no-nonsense spirit. In a society, a culture, and a literature

in which deference to all forms of authority is stressed and indirection is widely held to be the most appropriate mode of expressing one's thoughts and conducting one's affairs, or the only viable one, Botchan's unapologetic defiance of the constraints of family life and school routines, and his willingness to expose great and petty pretensions and skulduggeries wherever he finds them, regardless of the consequences, must resonate powerfully with readers who feel the same resentments but find themselves unable to act on them or even voice them.

These themes may also resonate with English-speaking readers who have already experienced similar satisfactions while reading *Huckleberry Finn* or *The Catcher in the Rye;* and for those without direct experience of Japanese life, they may also provide an eye-opening antidote to long-prevalent media (and academic) evocations of a harmonious, largely complacent social order. The same applies to Botchan's, or rather Natsume Sōseki's, child's-eye view of family life, which is shockingly cold and disconnected. No doubt there is an element of intentional exaggeration for maximum emotional impact here – but the same could just as easily be said of the more familiar evocation of childhood in a warm, enveloping atmosphere as celebrated in countless Japanese television series.

If *Botchan's* outspoken style and rebellious spirit are among the features that help account for its perennial appeal, other elements of the novel may now feel distinctly dated. Natsume Sōseki wrote in the last age of pre-Freudian literature. Living in the era we do, we can't help viewing his works, or most other things, from a Freudian (or post-Freudian) perspective, but it is still worth remembering that Sōseki himself did not have such a perspective. Neither did his original readers. Botchan, even by the standards of fictional characters in his own day, and in sharp contrast to later Sōseki protagonists, is rarely given to psychological introspection, or to any form of self-examination at all. Nor is he subject to the imperatives of the libido that we now take for granted; in fact he must be one of the few (presumably heterosexual) characters who seem immune to the supposedly irresistible charms of the geisha, although some of his colleagues prove far less innocent. The only female character for whom he expresses anything more than fleeting feelings is the elderly Kiyo, whose devotion makes her a kind of substitute mother figure rather than a candidate for a juicy seduction. No doubt this will detract from the overall sense of authenticity, or even the interest, of the novel for some readers.

Given the youthfulness of the main character, the weakness of his erotic impulses, and the setting of much of the action in a middle school, it may be tempting to read *Botchan* as a boys' book. Even if we focus on the more adult elements, especially the depiction of the intrigues among the teachers at the school which come to occupy center stage as the story progresses, its outlook is still very much a masculine one. Depictions of the female characters other than Kiyo are cursory, and their roles are largely limited to advancing a plot line that concentrates on the adventures, misadventures, and conflicts among the male characters. The same is true, in fact, of much of Sōseki's writing. Even in the deeper and more complex later novels, the male characters are the ones who generally make things happen and do most of the important thinking; female characters generally have things happen to them, and their thoughts are accorded less attention. Yet *Botchan* could not have enjoyed the kind of popularity it has without a good measure of favor among female readers as well; perhaps female readers, whose lives are hemmed in by the same social constraints as those of their male counterparts, plus some extra ones thrown in for good measure, also get a vicarious satisfaction out of Botchan's outspokenness and defiance of the rules.

Names, especially nicknames, play an important role in this novel. Botchan's real name is never mentioned. The one character with a real name that carries a clear symbolic value is the maid Kiyo ('Pure'), whose simplicity, naïveté, and unwavering devotion to Botchan are all explicitly linked to the values of the feudal society in which she was raised, and implicitly contrasted with the constant change and crass careerism of modern times.

The nicknames that Botchan gives to his colleagues at the school seem to be among the novel's most pleasing and memorable features for Japanese readers, who undoubtedly enjoy comparing them with the names that they came up with for their own teachers, and are also probably delighted to see a teacher getting in on the game himself. Each of these names carries some kind of specific association in Japanese, so a bit of explanation may be helpful.

Botchan's nickname for the Principal is Tanuki, an animal that resembles a raccoon but is commonly translated as 'badger'; in Japanese folklore it is known as a wily creature with the ability to deceive or bewitch humans.

The Assistant Principal's nickname is taken from the red flannel shirt that he habitually wears, an emblem of his aspiration to adopt a 'modern' way of life, or more precisely to affect some of the flashier accessories of modernity in an ultimately vain effort to conceal the hypocrisy, pettiness, and deviousness of his deeper nature.

Redshirt's sidekick, the art teacher Yoshikawa, is dubbed Nodaiko, a term that referred to flunkey-like entertainers who attached themselves to parties of pleasure seekers and provided a range of mood-enhancing services including flattery, jesting, and cajolery as the merrymakers wended their way from teahouse to restaurant to Kabuki playhouse to brothel. Since there is no term for this occupation in English (although real-life specimens undoubtedly do exist), the rather unsatisfactory approximation Hanger-on is used in the translation in the hope that it will convey at least a little sense of the frivolous and parasitic associations of the original.

The pasty-faced English teacher Koga becomes Uranari Hyōtan, a pale, puffy squash that grows at the end of a vine that has lost most of its vitality; while this seems to be another of Botchan's unflattering characterizations, he soon develops a deep respect for this hapless figure as one of the few examples of a man of integrity, a true gentleman, among his colleagues.

Botchan's pugnacious fellow mathematics teacher, Hotta, sports a bristly haircut and is assigned the nickname Yamaarashi (Porcupine). This is a creature without the clear-cut legendary associations of the Tanuki, but it suits Hotta's prickly, unyielding personality neatly.

Finally, there is the Madonna, the novel's only female character of consequence other than Kiyo. Her name, like Kiyo's, evokes a vision of idealized purity, but in her case the label proves to be all too ironic; in contrast to Kiyo's simple but strongly rooted virtues, the undeserved application of the Western name to this much younger woman suggests the fickleness and superficiality that Sōseki found so rampant in the rapidly modernizing Japan of his day.

The location of the school where the bulk of the story unfolds is invariably taken to be the city of Matsuyama on the island of Shikoku, a former feudal castle town turned provincial capital where Natsume Sōseki himself spent a year as a middle school teacher of English. (The students of that era, incidentally, spent five years in middle school, so Botchan is only a few years older than his students, and physically less imposing than some of them.) The Matsuyama dialect is echoed in the speech of the locals in the novel, including the distinctive phrase *na moshi* which Sōseki sprinkles liberally in dialogue passages. The city is adjoined by a celebrated hot spring resort, the fictional counterpart of which qualifies as one of the very few redeeming features of the place in Botchan's eyes. Despite his many unflattering comments about the backwardness and pettiness of provincial life – like his creator, Botchan takes great pride in his identity as an Edokko, a feisty, dashing native of the old shogunal capital that was renamed Tokyo when it became the seat of the new government in 1868 – Matsuyama's tourist industry goes on capitalizing happily on the novel's popularity. Sōseki, however, is careful never to name the city explicitly. Neither does he specify the war whose victorious conclusion is celebrated in Chapter 10; it is generally assumed to be the Russo-Japanese War, which ended in 1905, the year before *Botchan*'s first publication.

J. Cohn

BOTCHAN

I

From the time I was a boy the reckless streak that runs in my family has brought me nothing but trouble. Once when I was in elementary school I jumped out of one of the second-story windows and I couldn't walk for a week. Some people might wonder why I'd try such a daredevil stunt. It's not as if there was any special reason. I was just sticking my head out of a window in the new school building one day, and one of my classmates started making fun of me and saying that even though I acted tough I was really a sissy and I would never jump out that window. When the school custodian carried me home on his back, my old man was furious and said that he couldn't believe that somebody couldn't walk just because they'd jumped out of a second-story window. I told him that next time I tried that jump I'd walk away from it.

I had a nice imported knife that one of my relatives had given me, and once when I was holding it up to the sun to show my friends how shiny the blade was, one of them said that it was shiny all right but it probably wouldn't cut anything. I told him that it would cut through anything just fine and if he didn't believe me I would prove it. He dared me to try cutting my finger with it, so I said all right, just watch, and cut a diagonal slice across my right thumb. Luckily it was just a small knife and the bone was good and hard, so that thumb is still attached to my hand, but the scar will be there until the day I die.

About twenty paces from the east side of our house we had a little vegetable patch with a chestnut tree standing right in the middle. Those chestnuts meant more to me than life itself. When they started to get ripe I would be out the back door as soon as I woke up to pick them up so I could take them to eat at school. The yard on the west side of our garden belonged to a pawnbroker called Yamashiro-ya. He had a son named Kantarō who was about thirteen. Kantarō was a sissy, of course, but he used to climb over the wood-and-bamboo fence and steal our chestnuts. One evening I hid out in the shadows by the gate and finally caught him at it. He saw that I'd cut off his escape route, so he jumped me with everything he had. He was two years older than me, and even though he was a sissy he was strong. He tried to butt me in the chest with that big flat head of his, but all he managed to do was get it stuck in the sleeve of my kimono. I couldn't use my arm with his head stuck in my sleeve, so I just kept waving it around while his head flopped back and forth with it. When he couldn't take it any more he bit into my arm. That really hurt, so I pushed him against the fence and then I tripped him up and threw him over. Yamashiro-ya's property was six feet lower than our garden. Kantarō took a chunk out of the fence as he dropped back over into his own territory with a pathetic moan. My sleeve got torn off as he fell, so I could finally move my arm again. When my mother went over to apologize that night, she managed to get the sleeve back.

That wasn't all – I got into lots of other trouble as well. There was the time when I got together with Kane-kō the carpenter's son and Kaku the fish peddler's son and wrecked old Mosaku's carrot patch. He had left some straw spread out on a piece of ground where the carrots hadn't all come up yet, so the three of us used it as a sumo ring. We wrestled there for hours, and by the time we were through the carrots were all trampled flat. Another time I plugged up the water pipe in the Furukawas' rice paddy. They had a thick tube of hollowed-out bamboo buried deep in the ground with water coming out of it to irrigate the rice plants. I didn't know what it was there for, and one day I stuffed the opening full of rocks and twigs until the water stopped coming out. Later, when I was back home eating dinner, old Mr Furukawa burst in. He was yelling so hard he turned red in the face. As I recall, my parents had to pay him some money to make up for it.

My old man never showed any fondness for me, and my mother always favored my older brother. His face was so pale it was creepy, and he liked to act out scenes from Kabuki plays – especially the female roles. Every time the old man laid eyes on me he'd tell me that I'd never amount to much. My mother would tell me I was so rough that she worried about what would become of me. Well, it's true that I never have amounted to much. When you look at how things have turned out, it's no wonder that she was worried. I have managed to stay out of jail so far, but that's about as much as I can say for myself.

When my mother was sick, only two or three days before she died, I bumped against the stove while I was doing somersaults in the kitchen and bruised my ribs. It hurt like hell. My mother was furious and said that she never wanted to see my face again, so I went off to stay at a relative's place. Then the news came that she was dead. I never thought she would die so soon. If she was that sick, I really should have behaved better than I did. When I got home, my brother told me that I was a disgrace to the family and that it was because of me that Mother had died so quickly. I was so upset I smacked him in the face, which only got me into even more trouble.

After my mother died, I went on living with the old man and my brother. The old man was the kind of guy who never did anything himself, but all he had to do was catch sight of you and he'd be telling you how you were no good at all. I still can't figure out why he thought that way. One thing was for certain: I had a real character for an old man. My brother wanted to become a businessman and was always studying English. Anyway, he had that feminine streak and he was a sneak, so we didn't get along. Every ten days or so we'd get into a fight. One time when we were playing chess he caught me with a really sneaky move and then sat there gloating and rubbing it in while I squirmed. I was so mad that I grabbed one of the pieces and threw it at him. It hit him right between the eyes, hard enough to draw blood. He went to tell on me to the old man, who announced that he was going to disinherit me.

I figured that I was going to be disinherited just like he said and that was all there was to it, but then Kiyo, the old woman

who had been our maid for the last ten years, appealed to him
in tears, and he finally cooled down. Even with all this, though,
I wasn't particularly scared of the old man. Mainly I felt sorry
for Kiyo. According to the stories I heard she was supposed to
be from a respectable family, but when the shogunate was
overthrown she was left with nothing and ended up having to
work as a servant. That's why she was just a humble old woman
now. I don't know what kind of karmic link there was between
the two of us, but for some reason she was tremendously fond
of me. It was really amazing. My mother had had enough of
me three days before she died . . . the old man never had any
use for me at all . . . and everybody in the neighborhood
thought I was just a little good-for-nothing and wouldn't have
anything to do with me . . . but this one old woman was absolutely crazy about me. I had already come to the conclusion
that I wasn't the kind of person that anybody could like and
it didn't bother me at all if people treated me as if I was just a
block of wood, which only made me wonder all the more why
Kiyo fussed over me the way she did. Sometimes when she was
in the kitchen and nobody else was around, she would praise
me for having what she called 'a fine, upstanding character.' I
had no idea what she meant, though. I figured that if I really
had such a fine character, other people should be treating me
a little better. Whenever Kiyo said something like that, I'd tell
her that I couldn't stand being flattered. Then she'd say that it
just showed how fine my character really was, and gaze at me
adoringly. She seemed to be taking pride in some version of me
that she'd created all by herself. There was something almost
creepy about it.

Kiyo grew even fonder of me after my mother died. Sometimes in my child's heart I wondered why. I didn't appreciate it
and wished she would put a stop to it. I thought it was pathetic.
She kept right on spoiling me, though. Sometimes she would
take her own spending money and buy me various kinds of
sweets. On cold nights she'd slip out and buy some buckwheat
flour and after I'd gone to bed she'd come in and leave a steam-
ing bowl of gruel by my pillow. There were even times when
she'd buy me a pot of hot noodle stew. And it wasn't just food,

either: socks, pencils, notebooks – I got all kinds of presents from her. Another time – this was much later – she even gave me three yen and told me it was a loan. It wasn't as if I had asked her to lend me any money. She just brought it to my room and said that it must be hard for me without any spending money, so I should take it and use it to get something I wanted. I told her that I didn't need it, of course, but she insisted that I should take it, so that's what I did, and actually I was very glad to have it. I put the three one-yen bills in a purse, stuck it in my kimono – and then went off to the toilet, where I managed to drop it right down the hole. There was nothing I could do except come slinking back and explain to Kiyo what had happened. She immediately went and found a bamboo pole and told me that she'd fish it out for me. After a while I heard the sound of splashing water by the well, and when I went to see what was happening, there she was with the cord of my purse hanging from the tip of the pole, trying to rinse it off. When we opened it up, the bills were all faded and the paper was stained a brownish color. Kiyo dried them off over the hibachi and gave them back to me, saying that they should be all right now. I took a sniff. It was pretty bad, and I told her so. She said I should give them to her and she'd change them for me, and somehow or other she managed to get them exchanged for three silver one-yen coins. I can't remember what it was that I bought with those coins. I told her that I'd pay her back soon, but I never did. Now I wish I could pay her back ten-fold, but it's not possible any longer.

When Kiyo gave me these presents she would always be careful to choose times when the old man and my brother were not around. Now, there's nothing I hate more than getting something all to myself behind everybody else's back. It's true that I didn't get along with my brother, but that doesn't mean that I enjoyed being given sweets and colored pencils without his knowing about it. I asked Kiyo why she was always giving me stuff but never gave my brother anything. She replied with a straight face that our father would buy things for him, so he didn't need any presents from her. This wasn't really fair. The old man was hard-headed all right, but he wasn't the kind to play favorites like that. I guess it seemed that way to Kiyo, though. She must have been absolutely crazy about me. Even though she came from a good family, she had no education at all, so what could I do? That's not all there was to it, either. The kind of devotion she had for me was downright scary. She was absolutely certain I was going to have a glorious career and become a wonderfully distinguished man. My brother, on the other hand, had nothing going for him but his fair complexion, and would never amount to anything as far as she was concerned. She had simply convinced herself that people she liked were sure to be big successes, and people she didn't like were bound to fail, and there was absolutely no way you could talk her out of these notions. At that time I didn't have any particular ideas about what I was going to do with my life. But because Kiyo kept insisting that I was going to be somebody important, I gradually began to feel it might be true. It seems ridiculous when I think about it now. Once I actually asked her what she thought I would become, but it turned out that she didn't seem to have any more of an idea than I did. All she was certain of was that I'd travel around town in my own private rickshaw and get myself a house with a magnificent entrance.

What's more, Kiyo had a notion that once I was on my own and had that house, she should come and join me there. Over and over, she asked me to let her live with me. I myself had come to believe that I'd manage to end up with a house of my own somehow, so I told her I'd take her in. She had a tendency to let her imagination run wild, though, and sometimes she'd ask me whether I thought Kōjimachi was a more suitable neighborhood than Azabu, or tell me that it would be nice if we put a swing in the yard, or that one Western-style room would be plenty, as if she was getting it all planned out in advance. In those days I didn't have the least interest in things like owning a house. Western-style or Japanese, it wasn't something that I had any use for, so whenever Kiyo started in on her fantasies I would tell her that I didn't want any of that grand stuff. Then she would praise me again, saying that it just showed how unselfish I was, what a pure heart I had. No matter what I said, she could always find some reason to praise me for it.

We went on living this way for five or six years after my mother died, with me getting chewed out by the old man, getting into fights with my brother, and getting sweets and compliments from Kiyo. I never wished for anything more; things were fine with me just the way they were, and I figured that this must be more or less the way it was for other kids as well. Still, Kiyo kept telling me what a poor, unfortunate boy I was, and eventually I came to believe that I really was as unfortunate as she said. Other than that there was nothing that bothered me at all, except that the old man would never give me any pocket money.

In January of the sixth year after my mother's death, the old man had a stroke and died. That April I graduated from a private middle school, and in June my brother graduated from his business school. He took a job with some company, and was assigned to their office in Kyushu. I still had to finish my education in Tokyo. My brother announced that he was going to sell off the house and all our parents' possessions before heading off to Kyushu. I told him he could do whatever he wanted as far as I was concerned. No matter what, I didn't want to feel beholden to him for anything. And even if he did try to take care of me, I knew that he wouldn't miss a chance to use it against me when we got into a quarrel, which we were bound to do sooner or later anyway. I wasn't about to bow down to a brother like him just so I could get whatever help he might be willing to give me. I figured that there would always be something I could do to get by on my own – even if it meant that I'd have to work as a milkman, well, I was ready. My brother brought in a dealer in second-hand goods and sold off all the junk that had accumulated in our house from generation to generation for next to nothing. He got somebody to help him unload the house and land, and they managed to find a wealthy buyer. It seems that he made a lot of money off the deal, but I don't know any of the details. I had already moved out a month before and taken a room in a boardinghouse in Kanda until I could figure out my next move. Kiyo was very upset that the house she had been serving in for more than ten years was being let go, but it wasn't hers so there was nothing she could do about it. Over and over she lamented that if only I had been a little bit older I could have inherited the place myself. Of course, if I could have inherited it when I was a little older, I should have been entitled to inherit it just as easily right then. The old woman didn't understand how these things work at all, so she actually thought that getting older was all it took for you to inherit an older brother's property.

So my brother and I went our separate ways, but there was still the problem of where Kiyo should go. My brother was hardly in a position to take her with him, of course, and besides she didn't have the slightest interest in trailing along after him all the way out to Kyushu. But I was holed up in my nine-foot-square room in a cheap boardinghouse at that point, and for all I knew I might even be forced to get out at any time. There was nothing that either of us could do for her. Finally I put the question to Kiyo herself. When I asked if she was planning to go into service in some other house, she said that until I had a home of my own and got married, she had no choice but to move in with her nephew and that was what she'd decided to do. This nephew was a clerk in the courts, reasonably well off, and he had already invited Kiyo to come and live with him if she was so minded on a couple of occasions, but she'd always turned down the offer, saying that she preferred staying on in a place that she'd been used to for years, even as a maid. This time, though, she must have decided that moving in with him would be better than starting over as a servant in some unfamiliar household where she'd have to worry all the time about fitting in. Still, she said, I should get myself a house and a wife as soon as possible and she'd come and take care of me. She must have preferred me, even though I wasn't a flesh-and-blood relative, to her nephew who was one.

Two days before my brother left for Kyushu, he came around to my boardinghouse and presented me with six hundred yen. He said that I could use it as capital to set myself up in some business, or to pay for continuing my education – whatever I did with it was up to me, but I shouldn't expect anything more from him. By my brother's standards this was a pretty impressive move. It wasn't as if it would have bothered me if he hadn't given me the money, but I admired him for handling the situation like a man, so I accepted it and thanked him. Then he took out another fifty yen and told me to give it to Kiyo, which I gladly agreed to do. Two days later we said goodbye at Shinbashi Station, and I haven't seen him since.

Lying on my bedding, I thought about what to do with the six hundred yen. Going into business would be a real bother, and I wouldn't be able to make a go of it anyway, especially since it didn't seem very likely that you could set yourself up in any kind of decent business with only six hundred yen. Even if you could, the way the world is now you'd always be at a disadvantage unless you could present yourself in society as an educated man. Forget about using the money as capital; I'd study something, I decided, and use it for tuition. If I split it into three parts, I could study for three years, with two hundred yen to spend each year. If I gave it everything I had for three years I should be able to accomplish something. The next question to consider was what kind of school to go to, but I had never taken a liking to any of the subjects. Language and literature? Certainly not – when it came to stuff like modern poetry, I couldn't even understand one line out of twenty. I was thinking that it really didn't matter what field I chose since I was sure not to like it anyway, but then as luck would have it I happened to walk past the Institute of Physical Sciences and saw a sign saying STUDENTS WANTED. This, I figured, was meant to be, so I took a look at their list of regulations, and signed up right then and there. When I think about it now, I realize that this was another one of those blunders I owe to that reckless streak which runs in the family.

For three years I studied about as hard as everybody else, but I wasn't particularly good at it and if you looked for my name in the class rankings you would have had an easier time finding it if you started from the bottom. Still, incredible as it seemed, when the three years were up I managed to graduate. I couldn't help thinking that it was kind of odd, but since it wouldn't have made any sense to lodge a complaint, I accepted the diploma without protest.

Eight days after I graduated I was summoned by the headmaster. When I reported to his office, wondering what it was about, I was told that there was an opening for a mathematics teacher in a middle school somewhere out in Shikoku, paying forty yen a month. Was I interested? Well, the idea that I might become a teacher, or that I might go and live in the provinces, had never even occurred to me despite having just spent three years at my studies. But of course I didn't have any ideas about doing something *other* than teaching, either, so I agreed on the spot. Once again, that reckless streak did me in.

Since I had accepted the offer, I had to go. In the three years I'd been holed up in my nine-foot-square room I hadn't had to put up with a single critical remark. I hadn't gotten into any fights. Compared to what came before and after, it was a pretty carefree phase of my life. But now I'd have to leave my little room behind. The only time I had been out of Tokyo in my entire life was when I went on an excursion to Kamakura with some of my classmates. This time it would be nowhere as close by as Kamakura – I'd be going somewhere awfully far away. When I looked for it on a map, I saw that it was on the coast, no bigger than a pinpoint. It couldn't be much of a place. I didn't have a clue what the town or the people who lived there were like. That didn't matter, though. There was no point worrying. I would just go. All the same, it was kind of a bother.

I had gone to visit Kiyo a number of times since we had gotten rid of the old house. Her nephew turned out to be a surprisingly fine person. He would always go out of his way to be nice to me if he was at home when I visited. Kiyo would sing my praises to him – she would even announce that I was going to buy a mansion in Kōjimachi and get a good job with the government as soon as I graduated. Since she had taken it on herself to chart my life out this way, these conversations were kind of hard for me and all I could do was sit there and blush. And it wasn't only once or twice that this happened. Sometimes she would even talk about the way I wet my bed when I was little, which was enough to make me squirm. I don't know what the nephew was thinking as he listened to Kiyo carrying on like this. At any rate, she was an old-fashioned kind of woman, and she thought of our relationship in terms of the master-retainer relations of feudal times. She seemed to believe that if I was her master, then I ranked as her nephew's master as well. It must have been pretty embarrassing for him!

In due course it was officially confirmed that I had been hired. Three days before I set out, I went to see Kiyo, but she was down with a cold, lying in a little room on the north side of the house. When she saw me there it seemed to boost her spirits right away, and she sat up and asked when I was going to get a house of my own. She had this idea that all you had to do was graduate and the money would just start sprouting in your pocket. What was even more ridiculous was the way she was still calling me Botchan, even though in her mind I was now a man of substance, not some little boy. It would be no simple thing for me to get a house any time soon. When I told her I was going to the country, she looked terribly disappointed and kept stroking the loose hairs at her graying temples over and over again. I felt so sorry for her that I tried to cheer her up by saying 'I have to go, but I'll be back soon. I'll be back next year at summer vacation for sure.' She still had a funny look on her face, so I asked 'What kind of souvenir should I bring back for you? What would you like?' 'I'd like some of those sweets from Echigo that come wrapped in bamboo leaves,' she said. I had never heard of anything like that, and besides Echigo was in a different direction from where I was headed. When I replied that I didn't think they had those in the part of the country I was going to, she asked 'Which direction are you going, then?' 'West,' I said. Then she asked 'Past Hakone, or on this side?' I didn't know how to even begin to explain.

The morning I left she came to my room and helped out with all kinds of things. She gave me a canvas bag with a toothbrush, tooth powder, and a towel she'd bought in a shop on the way over. I told her I didn't need them, but she wouldn't take no for an answer. We rode to the station in two rickshaws, side by side. After I had boarded the train she stood there on the platform, gazing at me through the window. 'We may not see each other again. Please take very good care of yourself,' she said in a tiny voice. Her eyes were filled with tears. Mine weren't, but it was all I could do to keep myself from crying. Once the train started

to pick up speed I thought I would be all right and I stuck my
head out the window and looked back. She was still standing
there. Somehow she looked awfully small.

2

When the ship came to a stop with a blast from its whistle, a barge pulled out from the shore and was rowed over to us. The boatman was stark naked except for a red loincloth. What a barbaric place! Of course, he probably couldn't stand wearing a kimono in that searing heat. The sun beat down so fiercely that the water shone with a nasty glint to it. Just looking at it was enough to make your eyes swim. I asked the purser if this was where I was supposed to get off and he said it was. From the look of it the place was a fishing town about the size of the neighborhood of Ōmori in Tokyo. Who the hell did they think they were, sending me to a place like this? How was I supposed to stand it? Well, there was nothing I could do about it now. I jumped down onto the barge ahead of everybody else, and five or six people got on after me. They loaded a couple of big boxes on too and then Redloin rowed us in to the shore. When we landed I was again the first one to jump off. Right away I grabbed a runny-nosed kid who was standing there and asked him where the middle school was, but he just gawked at me and said 'I dunno.' The dim-witted hick! The whole town wasn't any bigger than a cat's forehead, so how could you not know where the middle school was? Just then a man in a strange-looking kimono with tight sleeves walked up and said 'Come with me' and when I followed along he led me to an inn called Minato-ya or something like that. A bunch of nasty-looking maids all joined voices to greet me, which just made me want to have nothing to do with the place. I stopped in the entryway and asked them where the middle school was. When they told me that it was a couple of miles away by train, I was even more determined not to stay here. I snatched my two valises from the guy in the tight-sleeved kimono and started walking. The people in the inn gave me a strange look.

I found the train station soon enough and bought myself a ticket. When I got on the train, it looked as dinky as a matchbox. It had hardly started to get rolling when it was already time to get off; the whole ride couldn't have taken more than five minutes. No wonder the ticket was so cheap, I thought – only three sen! I got into a rickshaw and set off for the middle school, but when I got there, classes were already over for the day and there was no one around. The custodian explained that the teacher on night duty had just gone out on an errand. For somebody who was supposed to be on night duty, he seemed to have a pretty casual attitude. I thought about paying a call on the Principal, but by this point I was already feeling so worn out that I just got back in the rickshaw and told the driver to take me to an inn. He dashed me off to a place called Yamashiro-ya – the same name as the pawnbroker's shop that Kantarō's family ran, which was kind of funny.

For some reason the maid showed me to a dark room beneath the stairway. It was so hot I couldn't stand it. When I told her I didn't want this room she replied that unfortunately all the others were occupied and walked away, leaving my valises just where she had dropped them. There was nothing I could do about it, so I went in and sat there sweating. Eventually they told me that the bath was ready, so I headed for the bathroom and plunged right in, but came out just as quickly. On my way back, I took a look around and noticed that there were actually plenty of nice, cool-looking rooms open. It was outrageous – what a pack of liars!! By and by, a maid came around with my dinner tray. The room was as hot as ever, but the food was a lot better than what they gave me in my old boardinghouse. As she was serving the meal, the maid asked me where I was from, and I told her. Tokyo must be a very nice place, she said. It sure is, I said. After I finished and the maid went back to the kitchen with my tray, I could hear some people laughing out loud. Since there was nothing worth staying up for in a place like this I went right to bed, but it wasn't that easy to fall asleep. The heat wasn't the only problem – it was noisy, too. The racket was five times worse than it had been at the boardinghouse. When I finally drifted off, I had a dream about Kiyo. She was wolfing down some of those Echigo sweets, bamboo-leaf wrappers and all. I told her that bamboo leaves are poisonous and she shouldn't be eating them, but she said no, this kind is good for you and went on devouring them. Dumbfounded, I started roaring with laughter. At this point I woke up. A maid was opening the shutters. The sky was just as wonderfully clear as it had been the day before.

I had been told that when you take a trip, you're supposed to tip; if you don't, people won't treat you the way you deserve. They must have stuck me in this dark little room because I didn't hand out any tips; my shabby-looking outfit, canvas valises, and imitation satin umbrella couldn't have helped either. As if this bunch of hicks had the right to look down their noses at anybody! Well, I'd show them: let them have a tip that would be sure to give them a nice big shock. No matter how unimpressive I might have looked to them, I had thirty yen left in my pocket from my savings when I set out from Tokyo, and after paying for the train and boat fare and the rest of my travel expenses I still had fourteen left. And now I'd have my salary coming in, so even if I let them have all fourteen it wouldn't be a problem. Country people are cheapskates; a five-yen tip would surely be enough to make their eyes pop. Just wait till you get a look at this, I thought, as I coolly went off to wash my face, and then went back to my room and waited. The same girl from last night brought in my breakfast. As she served it, she kept breaking into an obnoxious smirk. Outrageous! What did she think she was gawking at, some kind of stage show? Even a face like mine was a lot more impressive sight than hers was, that much was for sure. I had been intending to wait until after she was through serving to hand over my tip, but I was feeling so angry I just took out a five-yen bill right then and there and told her to take it to the office. She gave me a strange look. After I finished breakfast I set out for the school right away. My shoes had been left unshined.

I had a pretty clear idea of how to get to the school since I had gone there in the rickshaw the day before. Just a couple of turns and I was right at the gate. The pathway from the gate to the school entrance was paved with slabs of granite, and the noise the rickshaw made as it rattled over them had been hard to take. As I was walking along I had seen lots of students in their heavy black uniforms; now they were all streaming through this gate. Some of them were taller than I was, and they looked stronger, too. When it hit me that I was supposed to be teaching kids like them, it made me feel kind of uneasy. I presented my name card and was ushered into the Principal's office. The Principal had a thin mustache, a dark complexion, and big eyes that made him look like a badger. His manner was horribly stuffy. He urged me to do my best and then solemnly handed me a Certificate of Appointment with a huge seal stamped on it. (Later, when I was on the boat on my way back to Tokyo, I took this certificate, crumpled it up, and pitched it into the sea.) Next, he told me that he was going to present me to the rest of the teaching staff, and that I should display my Certificate personally to each of them. What a lot of bother! It would have been less trouble just to hang it up in the faculty room for a couple of days.

The entire faculty wouldn't be assembling in the staff room until the first-period bugle sounded, which wouldn't be for a while yet. The Principal pulled out his pocket watch, gave it a glance, and announced that he planned to have a long, leisurely talk with me later on, but to begin with he wanted me to understand the main points in a general way; then launched into a lengthy discourse on the Spirit of Education. I just stood there more or less taking it in, of course, but as he droned on I began to think that I had let myself in for a lot of trouble by coming here. There was no way I could do what this Principal was expecting. Telling a reckless character like me that I was to be a role model for the students, and that I would be required to conduct myself in such a way that I would be looked up to by everyone in the school, and that a true educator is one who not only imparts knowledge but exerts a positive moral influence in his personal life – this was asking for a lot more than he had any reasonable right to expect. Did he really think that anyone of such distinction was going to come all the way out to some country town like this for forty yen a month? It had always seemed to me that all people are pretty much the same, and if something gets them angry enough they're bound to get themselves into a fight or two. At this rate, though, I'd just have to hold my tongue; in fact, I could hardly even go out for a walk! If the assignment was so demanding, they should have explained exactly what was involved before they'd hired me. I don't like lying, so there was no way out of it: I just had to face the fact that I'd come here based on a misapprehension, and make up my mind to give up the job and head for home right away. Now that I'd given the people at the inn that five-yen bill, all I had left was nine yen and change – not enough to get me back to Tokyo. What a blunder that tip had been! Even with only nine yen, though, things would work out one way or another. Even if it wasn't enough to cover my trip home, it was still better than lying.

When I informed the Principal that I couldn't possibly live up to the expectations he had for me and was therefore returning my Certificate of Appointment, he blinked those badger eyes of his and gazed into my face for a few moments. Then he laughed and said that what he had been talking about before was simply his ideal, and he was well aware that I wouldn't be able to live up to it so there was no need for me to worry. Well, if he was so sure of this all along, why did he have to intimidate me with that speech to begin with?

By and by the bugle sounded and we could hear a wave of boisterous noise from the classrooms. The Principal said that the teachers should all be assembled in the faculty room by now, so I followed behind him and went in. They were all sitting at their desks, which were lined up along the walls of the long, narrow room. As soon as I entered they all turned to look at me, as if by some prearranged agreement. Did they think I was going to put on some kind of show for them? I went around to each one, presented my Certificate for their inspection, and delivered a formal greeting, just as I had been instructed to do. Most of them just rose a little out of their seats and bowed, but some took the ceremony more seriously and actually accepted the Certificate when I offered it to them, made a show of reading it over, and solemnly handed it back. It felt as if everybody was just play-acting. By the time I got around to the fifteenth one – the physical education teacher – I was beginning to feel a bit on edge from having delivered the same greeting over and over again. Each of them only had to do this once, but I had to repeat it fifteen times. They should have tried giving a little thought to how it felt for the other person!

One of the people I greeted as I was making my rounds was the Assistant Principal, but I didn't catch his name. This Mr Something-or-Other was supposed to be a Bachelor of Arts, a genuine university graduate, which meant that he had to be an important person. He spoke in a gentle voice that had a strangely feminine tone to it. What really surprised me, though, was the flannel shirt he was wearing, despite the heat. No matter how thin the fabric might have been, it must have felt terribly warm. Leave it to a university graduate to go above and beyond the call like that, I guess. What's more, it was a red shirt – much too fancy for the likes of us. Later I found out that this fellow wore a red shirt all year round. This was a strange case! According to him, wearing red was good for your health, so he got these shirts of his made to order. He shouldn't have bothered – after all, if wearing red was so good for you, you might as well make your whole outfit red! Then there was the English teacher, named Koga, who had a terribly greenish, sickly-looking complexion. Pasty-faced people usually tend to be on the slim side, but this fellow's face had a puffy look. When I was a kid in grade school, I had a classmate called Tami-san whose old man had the same kind of coloring. He was a farmer, so one day I asked Kiyo if that was what happened to you if you became a farmer. She said it wasn't; the problem, she explained, was that he was always eating the pale squashes that grow right at the tip of the vine when the plant is past its prime, and that's how he got so pale and puffy-looking himself. Ever since then, whenever I've seen someone with a pasty, puffy face like that I've figured that they must have gotten that way by eating those squashes. This English teacher must have been eating a load of them, too. Actually, I still don't really understand what makes those squashes pale; when I asked Kiyo about it again she just laughed. I guess she didn't really know either. Next was the other mathematics teacher, whose name was Hotta. He was a rugged-looking fellow with short, bristly hair and a face that could have belonged to one of the rougher customers among the warrior monks of old. He didn't even bother to glance at the Certificate that I was politely holding out to him; instead he said 'Oh, so you're the new guy, are you? Well, come on over to my place sometime,' and gave me a big, hearty laugh. I couldn't see what was so funny. Who did he think would want to hang around with the likes of him if he was going to act so rude? I decided to call him the Porcupine because of the way his hair stood up. The Chinese classics teacher, as you might expect, was a stiff, formal type: 'Having only arrived yesterday, I fear you must be rather fatigued. And then to commence instruction immediately – most commendable!' There was something kind of charming about the way the old fellow rambled on. The art teacher looked like some bit player out of a theatrical company – sheer silk jacket over his kimono, flicking at the air with his fan. 'And where, my good man, might you be from? Tokyo? Ah, splendid, now I won't be so alone: I'm not ashamed to say I'm a Tokyo native myself . . .' If this is what passes for a Tokyo man, I thought to myself, I would rather have been born someplace else. I could fill you in with the same kinds of details for all the others, but I wouldn't know where to put an end to it, so I'll just stop here.

Once the formalities were more or less over, the Principal told me that that would do for today, and I should assume my duties in two days after having duly consulted with the head mathematics instructor about curricular matters. When I asked who this was, I was informed that it was the Porcupine, whom I've already mentioned. Damn it – this is the guy that I'd have to work under? Oh no! I could feel my heart sinking. 'Where are you staying?' the Porcupine asked. 'Yamashiro-ya? All right, I'll stop by soon and we can talk things over.' Before I could reply he grabbed his chalk and strode out the door toward his classroom. Any head instructor who would go to pay a call on his subordinate couldn't have much of a sense of appropriate behavior. Still, I had to admire him for not standing on ceremony.

At that point I was going to just go back through the school gate and head right back to my inn, but since there wasn't anything special for me to do when I got there, I decided to take a little stroll around the town instead, with no particular destination in mind. I saw the prefectural government building. It was an old one, left over from another era. I also saw the local army barracks. They weren't as impressive as the Azabu barracks back in Tokyo. I took a look at the main street. It was only about half as broad as the one in Kagurazaka, and the buildings were a lot less impressive, too. This was supposed to have been a pretty big castle town in the old days, but you really couldn't expect much from such a place. As I walked along feeling sorry for all the locals who were so proud to be residents of a castle town, I suddenly found myself back in front of Yamashiro-ya. The town wasn't as big as it might have seemed. I had probably already seen just about everything there was to see. I went inside, ready for lunch. As soon as she saw me in the entryway, the lady who ran the establishment jumped up from the front counter where she'd been sitting and welcomed me back with a bow so low that her head touched the floor. As I took my shoes off and stepped into the lobby, a maid appeared and took me up to the second floor where, she said, a good room was now available. Not only was it on the second floor, it was a fifteen-mat room, fifteen feet by eighteen, on the front side of the building, with an imposing alcove. Never in my life had I been in such a fancy room before. Thinking that there was no telling when I might have another chance to stay in another one like it, I immediately took off my suit, changed into a thin robe, and lay down right in the middle of the room with my arms and legs stretched out as wide as they would go. It felt wonderful!

After lunch I wrote a letter to Kiyo. I'm not much good at putting phrases together and I can't remember how to write a lot of the words, so I hate writing letters. It's not like there had ever been anybody that I had to write to, either, but I knew that Kiyo must be worrying about me. I wouldn't want her to think that I had drowned in a shipwreck or anything, so I gave it everything I had and wrote her a good long one. This is what it said:

I got here yesterday. It's a nothing place. I'm staying in a 15-mat room. I gave them a 5-yen tip and the lady who runs the place bowed down so low she scraped her forehead on the floor. Last night I couldn't get to sleep. I dreamed that you were eating those sweets, bamboo-leaf wrappers and all. I'll be back next summer. Today I went to school and I gave all the teachers nicknames. The Principal is the Badger. The Assistant Principal is Redshirt. The English teacher is the Pale Squash, the other math teacher is the Porcupine, and the art teacher is the Hanger-on. I'll write you more about it later. Goodbye!

I was feeling nice and relaxed after I finished my letter, so I stretched out on the floor in the middle of the room again and drifted off to sleep. This time I slept really soundly, no dreams at all. I only woke up when I heard somebody bellowing 'Is this the room?' and saw the Porcupine walk in. Before I was even completely awake, he was already getting the proceedings under way: 'Sorry about this morning. Now, your classes are . . .' At first I was so stunned I could hardly follow what he was saying, but as I listened I realized that the classes he was assigning me didn't sound particularly difficult, so I just went along with it. If that was all there was to it, he could have asked me to start right in the next day, never mind the day after. Once that was settled he announced, as if he had the whole thing worked out already, that I obviously couldn't be planning on staying at this inn very long, and that he knew a good place to stay where they wouldn't rent a room to just anybody but if he put in a good word for me they'd be sure to take me in, so I should get ready to move right away. It would be a good idea to have a look at the place today and get going as soon as possible, he added, so that I could get moved in the next day before my teaching duties began. It was true that I couldn't hope to stay on in this fancy room indefinitely; it might cost more than my whole salary for all I knew. It was too bad that I'd have to leave so soon after laying out that five yen tip. But since I was going to leave eventually anyhow it made sense to leave right away and get settled into a new place, so I asked the Porcupine to make the arrangements. He told me that I should go along with him and have a look, so I did. It was a very quiet place, on the side of a hill at the edge of town. The owner was an antiques dealer who went by the name of Ikagin; his wife looked to be a couple of years older than he was. When I was in middle school I had learned the word 'witch' in English class, and this lady looked just like one. Even if she was a witch, of course, it wasn't me that she was married to, so I didn't mind. We settled it that I would move in the next day. On the way back to the inn the Porcupine treated me to a dish of shaved ice. When I'd first met him at school I'd thought he was awfully rude and arrogant, but now that I saw him doing these things for me, he didn't seem so bad after all. I guess it was just that he was impulsive, plus he had a temper – the same as me. Later I heard that he was the most popular teacher with the students.

3

Finally it was time to head to school. The first time I walked into a classroom and stood up on the raised platform in front of the blackboard it felt kind of funny. As I went through my lecture, I was wondering to myself if maybe someone like me might actually make it as a teacher after all. The pupils were a rowdy bunch. Now and then one of them would shout out 'Sir!' in a voice that was ridiculously loud. That shook me a little. I had addressed my teachers the same way every day at the Institute of Physical Sciences, but there's a world of difference between calling your teachers 'Sir' and hearing students call you that. It gave me a sort of creepy-crawly feeling in the soles of my feet. I'm not a sneaky person, and I'm no coward, either, but unfortunately my nerves aren't as steady as they might be. Each time I was hit by one of those voices shouting 'Sir!' it made me feel the way I did back when I'd hear the noontime cannon suddenly boom out on the Imperial Palace grounds and I was on an empty stomach. I managed to get through the first class all right, but I didn't have to handle any particularly tough questions. When I went back to the faculty room, the Porcupine asked me how it went. I just nodded, which seemed to be good enough for him.

When I took my chalk and headed out for the second class, I felt as if I was marching off into enemy territory. In this class all the kids were bigger than me. Being a real Tokyo native, I have a slight build, plus I'm on the short side, so even when I stood up on that teacher's platform I couldn't say that I looked very imposing. When it comes to fighting I'm ready to take on anybody, even a sumo wrestler, but if you put me in front of a class of forty big squirts and ask me to keep them in line just by wagging my tongue, well, that's beyond me. But I reckoned that if I showed any weakness in front of these hicks they'd never let up on me, so I let them have my lecture as loud as I could make it, with a dash of Tokyo accent thrown in for good measure. At first they looked dazed, as if they were lost in a fog. Now I had them where I wanted them, so I decided to pour on a little more and started throwing in some tough-sounding Tokyo slang, at which point the kid sitting right in the middle of the front row, the strongest-looking kid in the whole class, suddenly stood up and said 'Sir!!' Here we go, I thought. When I asked him what he wanted, he said, 'Well, umm, when you talk so fast it's hard to understand, umm, could you slow down just a little bit if you don't mind – *na moshi*.' This 'if you don't mind *na moshi*' sounded awfully wishy-washy to me. All right, I said, if this is too fast for you I'll talk slower, but I'm from Tokyo and I can't talk the way you do; if you can't understand, just bear with it until you can.

Taking this approach I got through the second class more easily than I expected. But then as I was almost out the door one of the students came up to me with a geometry problem and said 'Could you show me how to solve this problem if you don't mind – *na moshi*.' It was so hard I didn't have a clue. I broke into a cold sweat. All I could do was tell him that I couldn't figure it out on the spot but I'd explain it next time, and get out of there in a hurry. Before I could escape, though, the boys started squealing with delight, and I could hear some of them chanting 'He can't do it! He can't do it!' The damned fools! Of course I couldn't solve a problem that hard, even if I was their teacher! What's so funny about saying you can't do it if you really can't? If I was good enough to figure out a problem like that, why would I have come all the way out here to the sticks for a measly forty yen a month? When I went back to the faculty room and the Porcupine asked me how the class had gone, I nodded again, but this time it wasn't enough of a report, so I told him that the students in this school seemed like a pretty thick-headed crew. He gave me a strange kind of look.

The third class, the fourth, and the one in the afternoon all

proceeded in more or less the same way. In each of my classes
that first day, something or other went slightly wrong. I realized
that being a teacher isn't nearly as easy as it looks. I had made
it through all my classes for the day, but I couldn't go home yet.
I would have to sit around waiting, with my mind a blank, until
three o'clock. Then, I'd been informed, I would have to do an
inspection of my homeroom after the students had finished cleaning it. I would also have to go over my attendance lists. Only
then would I be free to go home. Just because you've sold yourself for a salary, does that give them the right to make you sit
around with nothing to do, just staring at your desk? But if
everybody else was willing to put up with these rules without
complaining, I realized, it would hardly do for a newcomer like
me to raise a fuss, and so I just sat there too. As we were leaving,
I vented my frustration to the Porcupine: 'You know, it's ridiculous that they make us stay till three, no matter what.' At first
he just said 'Yeah, it's true,' and laughed, but then he turned
serious and added a warning: 'Look, you'd better not complain
too much about this school. And if you do, make sure you only
do it to me. There are some pretty strange people around here.'
We parted ways at a corner before there was time for me to hear
any more.

When I got home, the landlord came into my room and asked
if I'd like him to make some tea. I thought he meant that he
was going to offer me some of his own, but instead he took
mine, and helped himself to a cup into the bargain. For all I
knew, he may have been inviting himself to enjoy my tea while
I was off at school as well. He explained that he had always
been interested in antiques, and so eventually he had started to
do some dealing in a private way. 'I sense that you are a gentleman of quite sophisticated tastes. How would you like to start
a little collection of your own, just for fun?' Not on your life!
It was true that once a couple of years ago I'd been mistaken
for a locksmith at the Imperial Hotel when I had gone there on
an errand. Another time, when I was walking around near the
Great Statue of the Buddha in Kamakura wearing a blanket
over my head, one of the rickshawmen started addressing me
as 'Boss.' I had been taken for plenty of other things as well

over the years, but nobody had ever accused me of being a gentleman of quite sophisticated tastes before! You can usually tell everything you need to know about people from the way they look, or what they're wearing. I've seen what a man of sophisticated tastes is supposed to look like in those old ink paintings: they're wearing some kind of monk's cowl, or holding a slip of paper so they'll always be ready to dash off a poem. Anybody who tried to put me in that category with a straight face would have to be a really suspicious character. I told him that as far as I was concerned collecting antiques was a pastime best left to idle old men, and I had no use for it. He laughed and said no, it's true that nobody starts out with an interest in it, but once people develop a feel for it they rarely turn back. Meanwhile he poured himself some more of my tea and drank it with a peculiar flourish. I had actually asked him to buy some tea for me the night before, but this was awful stuff, bitter and thick. A single cup was enough to make your stomach feel funny. When I asked him to look for something less bitter next time he said 'Yes sir,' and helped himself to yet another serving, tipping the pot and holding it there long enough to make sure that he had squeezed out whatever last drops of flavor were left in the leaves. That's the kind of guy he was: as long as it was somebody else's tea, he was going to drink as much of it as he could. After he left, I did a little preparation for the next day's classes and then went to bed.

The days began to take on a regular pattern: walk to school in the morning, do my job, then come back to my room, where my landlord would soon drop in and ask if I'd like some tea. After a week of this I had a pretty good idea of what was what at school, and also of what kind of people the landlord and his wife were. I had heard from some of the other teachers that for their first week or month on the job they had been very worried about whether they were making a good impression or not, but that wasn't the way I felt at all. When I made mistakes in class I would feel bad about it, but after thirty minutes or so I had forgotten about it completely. I'm not the kind of guy who can worry about things for long even if I try. I was completely unconcerned with the effect my slip-ups in class might have on the students, or with what the Principal and Assistant Principal might think. Like I said before, my nerves aren't that steady, but once I take a stand I'll stick to it. I was ready to pack up and leave at any time if things didn't work out at this school, so the Badger and Redshirt didn't faze me at all. And as for those kids in my classes, I was even less tempted to bother with trying to keep on their good side. This approach worked fine at school, but at home things weren't so simple. If it was just the landlord dropping in to drink up my tea it wouldn't have been so bad, but he kept bringing various stuff to show me. First it was a bunch of things he called 'inzai' or some such name, little bars of stone that you could carve a seal on; he laid out about ten of them and said that he'd give me the lot for the bargain price of three yen. Since I wasn't some kind of second-rate journeyman artist who needed a bunch of fancy seals to make his work look good I had no use for them, and I told him so; then he unrolled a hanging scroll, a traditional-style bird and flower picture, and told me it was painted by a man named Kazan or something like that. He hung it up in the alcove himself, and asked 'Don't you think it's a splendidly executed piece?' I guess so, I said, just to say something, at which point he launched into a long-winded explanation of how there were two painters named Kazan – Something-or-other Kazan and another Something-or-other Kazan – and this scroll was by one of the Something-or-other Kazans and not the other. Then he urged me to buy it, adding that just for me he'd bring the price down to fifteen yen. When I told him that I didn't have that kind of money, he said it was no problem, I could pay whenever it suited me. The man simply wouldn't take no for an answer. I finally got rid of him by telling him that I wouldn't buy it even if I did have the money. Another time he lugged in a giant inkstone, as big as a gargoyle roof tile, and announced 'This is a Tankei stone, a Tankei.' Before he could repeat himself again, I decided to play dumb and asked him what a Tankei was, but that only got him started on another lecture. The inkstones of Tankei, he explained, were quarried from three different veins of rock: upper, middle, and lower. All of the stones on the market these days were from the upper level, but this one was a genu-

ine middle-level stone. 'Just look at these eyes,' he said, pointing
to some lighter spots in the blackish stone. 'You won't see many
specimens with three eyes like this. Feels absolutely superb when
you glide your ink stick over it. Please, go ahead, give it a try.'
As he shoved the thing in front of me I asked him what the price
was. 'The owner brought it back with him from China and he
says he's very eager to sell it, so I think we could let you have
it for only thirty yen.' The man must have been out of his mind.
At school it was looking like I'd be able to get by somehow or
other, but there was no way I could hold up much longer under
this trial by antiques.

Before long school started to become a problem too. One
evening while I was taking a stroll in a neighborhood called
Ōmachi, I saw a little shop next to the Post Office with a sign
that said TOKYO BUCKWHEAT NOODLES. I love buckwheat
noodles. When I was in Tokyo, just passing a noodle shop and
getting a whiff of the spicy, simmering broth was enough to
make me want to dash right in. Now, with my head stuffed with
mathematics and antiques, I had forgotten all about noodles,
but once I caught sight of that sign I just couldn't pass it by, so
I decided to go right in and have a bowl. As I looked around
inside, I saw that the sign had gotten my hopes up in vain. Since
it said TOKYO, you'd expect a slightly more decent-looking place;
maybe they didn't know what they were doing, or maybe they
didn't have the money to fix it up, but anyway it was horribly
filthy. The floor mats had turned brown with age, and there was
so much dirt rubbed into them that they had a scratchy feel. The
walls were black with soot. The ceiling was stained with smoke
from kerosene lamps and, even worse, it was so low that I found
myself keeping my head down all the time without even thinking about it. The only thing that looked brand new was the price
list hanging on the wall, with the names of the different dishes
written out in a flowery hand. It looked as though they must
have bought a dilapidated old building and just opened for business a couple of days ago. The first item on the list was tempura
noodles. 'Give me a bowl of the tempura,' I shouted. As soon as
I ordered, a group of three customers over in the corner, who
up to that point had been slurping away at their own noodles,

all turned to look at me. I hadn't noticed before – it was so dark in there – but when our eyes met I realized that they were all students from the school. They all bowed by way of greeting, so I did the same. The noodles were good and it had been a long time since I'd had any, so I polished off four bowls, all with tempura.

The next day I walked into my classroom just as I would any other day, only to find that someone had written the words MISTER TEMPURA in giant letters on the blackboard. As soon as the students saw me they burst into raucous laughter. The whole thing seemed so stupid, I asked them what was so funny about somebody eating tempura. One of them answered: 'But four bowls is too much, na moshi.' I told them that as long as I paid for them and I ate them, it wasn't any of their business if I had four bowls, five, or any other number I wanted. Then I rushed through my lecture and headed straight back to the faculty room. When I got to the next class ten minutes later, I found another message on the board: FOUR BOWLS OF TEMPURA – LAUGHTER STRICTLY PROHIBITED. The first time around I hadn't minded that much, but this time I was really upset. When you overdo a joke it just becomes obnoxious. It's like overcooking a rice cake until it gets all charred and tough: you can hardly expect anybody to be impressed. But country people haven't figured out this principle, and they seem to think that it's okay to keep pouring it on indefinitely. I guess if you live in a town so small that once you've walked around it for an hour there's nothing more to see, the sight of somebody eating some tempura seems like a big deal, right up there with the War with Russia, just because people don't have anything better to talk about. Absolutely pathetic! Considering the way they've been brought up, it's no wonder they turn into such small-minded twerps, depressingly stunted like bonsai maple trees in their little pots. If it was all just for fun I'd be laughing right along with them, but this was too nasty to be treated as innocent kid stuff. First I erased the board without saying a word. Then I turned to the class and asked them if they really thought this kind of stunt was funny. It was a downright despicable prank – if that word meant anything to them. At that point one of the kids stood up and said 'Isn't it despicable when you get mad just because somebody is laughing at you, na moshi?' What a bunch of losers they were! When I thought to myself that I had come all the way from Tokyo just to teach the likes of them, I felt disgusted. I warned them not to try any back talk and to get to work, and finally I got the lesson under way. In the next class, the blackboard said EATING TEMPURA MAKES A MAN TOUCHY. Things were really getting out of hand now. I was so furious that I announced that I refused to teach such an impudent crew and sailed right out of the room. The students, I was told later, were thrilled to have the class canceled. At this rate, I thought, I'd rather put up with the antiques than with that school.

By the time I had gone home and had a good night's sleep, I wasn't feeling so worked up about the incident any more. The students were all sitting in their places that morning as if nothing had happened. It just didn't make sense. Everything went smoothly enough for the next three days, but on the evening of the fourth day I went and had some dumplings in a place called Sumida. This was a hot-spring area, about ten minutes from town by train or thirty minutes on foot. Along with the inns, restaurants, and a park, there was also a red-light district there. I had heard about a shop at the edge of the red-light district that served very good dumplings, so on my way back from the bathhouse I decided to stop in and give them a try. This time there were no students around so I figured that nobody would hear about it, but when I went into my first class the next morning, there on the board was TWO PLATES OF DUMPLINGS, SEVEN SEN. In fact, I did have two plates and I did pay seven sen. What a pain these kids were! The second class, I was sure, would come up with something too, and so it did: DUMPLINGS IN THE RED-LIGHT DISTRICT – YUM YUM! It was simply beyond belief. That was the end of the dumplings, but before I knew it they'd found something else: my red towel. This one was really stupid. I had gotten into the habit of going for a daily bath in the hot spring at Sumida. Unlike everything else around there, which wasn't even close to measuring up to what we had in Tokyo, this place was really first class. I figured that since it was so close by I might as well treat myself to a bath there every day, so before my dinner I would take a walk out to Sumida, which gave me some exercise into the bargain. On these walks I always carried a big bath towel. Now this towel took on a reddish tint from the water, and the dye from its red stripes began to run as well, so from a distance you might think it was solid red. Coming and going, on foot or by train, I always had that towel in my hand – and so, I heard, the students had taken to calling me Red Towel. Living in a little town where everybody knows everybody's business is no fun! And that wasn't all. The baths were in a newly built three-story building. If you went in the First Class Bath they gave you a cotton bathrobe and an attendant would scrub your back for you, all for eight sen, and a girl would serve you a bowl of green tea on an elegant Chinese-style stand. I always went First Class. When the kids got wind of this, they spread the word that bathing First Class every day was extravagant for a teacher on a salary of forty yen – as if I needed that kind of advice! And *that* wasn't all, either. The bath itself was a huge granite-lined tub, about fifteen feet by eighteen. Usually there would be a dozen or so people soaking in it, but sometimes I had it all to myself. The water was about chest-high, and it felt really nice to get a little exercise by taking a swim in it. I would keep an eye out for moments when the coast was clear, and then I'd have myself a great time splashing around. But then one day when I hurried down from the third floor to the bath, hoping that I'd be lucky enough to enjoy a good swim, there was a big sign with the warning SWIMMING IN THE BATH STRICTLY PROHIBITED in bold black lettering. There couldn't have been many other people who swam in that bath, so they must have put up the sign just for me. I didn't try to swim any more after that. But what really surprised me was that the next day at school, there on the board was the message SWIMMING IN THE BATH STRICTLY PROHIBITED. It seemed as if the whole student body was intent on keeping me under surveillance like a pack of detectives. It was downright depressing. No matter what they said about me it wasn't going to make me stop doing what I wanted to do, but when I wondered what had made me come to such a petty, narrow-minded kind of place I felt completely disgusted. And then when I went back home I had to put up with the usual trial by antiques again.

4

Everyone on the staff had to take turns doing night duty at the school – everybody, that is, except for the Badger and Redshirt. When I asked why these two were excused from this obligation, the answer was that they, unlike the rest of us, were directly appointed to their positions by the Prime Minister. It was ridiculous: they had the biggest salaries and worked the shortest hours, and on top of that they got out of doing night duty – how unfair could you get? First they come up with some arbitrary rule, then they go around acting as if it's only natural. Of all the nerve! I was really upset about it, but according to the Porcupine no matter how long a list of grievances I came up with I wouldn't be able to do anything about them. You'd think that as long as they were legitimate you *should* be able to do something about them, even if you were only a minority of one or two. The Porcupine used an English expression, 'Might is right,' to make his point, but I wasn't sure what the point was supposed to be, so he explained that it meant that the people with the power get their way. That principle I already knew; I hardly needed the Porcupine to deliver a lecture on the subject. But that was a whole different issue from night duty. How could anybody respect the 'power' of people like the Badger and Redshirt? Anyway, regardless of this debate, my turn to do night duty came around eventually. Now, being the high-strung type that I am, I just can't get a good night's sleep if I don't sleep in my own bedding. Even when I was a kid, I hardly ever slept over with my friends. Since I could barely stand to sleep at my friends' places, I felt even worse about spending the night at school. But no matter how bad I felt, this was part of what they were paying me those forty yen for, so I just had to tough it out.

Once the other teachers and the day students had gone home, there was nothing for me to do but sit around by myself, which felt kind of silly. The night duty room was on the west end of the dormitory building, behind the building where the classrooms were. The late afternoon sun was pouring in full blast, and from the moment I went in it was so hot I couldn't stand it. Even though the summer was over, the heat took its time out here in the country, just like everything else. I had one of the dinners they gave the students brought in; I could hardly believe how awful it was. It was amazing that they had the energy to run around the way they did on a diet of that kind of stuff. What's more, they made such quick work of it that they were all done by half past four – you really had to take your hat off to them! It was still light out when I finished dinner, so going to bed was obviously out of the question. Suddenly I got the urge to pay a visit to the hot spring. I wasn't sure whether it was all right to leave the premises when you were on night duty, but the idea of sitting around there staring off into space like a prisoner in solitary confinement was more than I could bear. I'd thought it was strange when I had asked for the night duty teacher that first time I came to the school and the custodian had told me that he was out running an errand, but now that it was my turn I could see why. Better to go. I told the custodian that I was going out for a little while, and when he asked me if it was on business I said no, I was going to the hot spring, and went on my way. Unfortunately I had left my red towel at home, but I could always rent one at the bathhouse.

I took my time and had a nice, leisurely soak. I finally took the train back to town just as evening was coming on and headed back to school, which was a couple of hundred yards from the station. Just when I was thinking that everything had worked out fine, I noticed the Badger walking down the street toward me. He must have been planning to take the train to the hot spring himself. He was moving along at a pretty brisk pace, but as we passed each other he realized it was me, so I gave him a quick bow. 'Ah, now as far as I can recall, weren't you supposed to be on duty tonight?' he asked in an official-sounding tone. There was no need for him to be coy about it – he knew full well that only two hours earlier he had walked over to me and said 'Ah, tonight's your first turn on night duty, isn't it?' and thanked me in advance. It seemed as if expressing yourself in this annoyingly roundabout way was one of the job requirements for being a Principal. Now I was good and angry, so I simply announced 'Yes, sir, I am on night duty. And that is why I am on my way to school, which is where, you may be certain, I will be spending the night.' Then I turned on my heel and walked away. But when I got to the corner at Tatemachi it was the Porcupine's turn to cross my path. This really was a small town – all you had to do was head out the door and you'd be sure to run into somebody or other.

'Hey, aren't you on night duty?' he asked. 'Yeah, I am,' I said. 'Well,' he went on, 'don't you think it's improper for the night duty teacher to go out for a stroll?' 'Not at all,' I said, with a show of dignity. 'In fact, it would be improper *not* to go out for a stroll.' 'You could get yourself into some real trouble with that kind of attitude, you know – especially if you happen to run into the Principal or the Assistant Principal,' he said. That was hardly the kind of thing I expected to hear from the Porcupine of all people, so this time I let him have it: 'Well, in fact I just *did* run into the Principal. And he said it was a good idea to go out for a walk, because if you didn't, night duty would be an awful grind when it's so hot.' Then, since there was no point in talking about it any further, I turned and walked back to school.

It wasn't long before the sun went down. After it got dark I invited the custodian into my room for a chat, but after a couple of hours of talking about this and that I'd had enough. Even though I wasn't sleepy yet I decided I might as well turn in. I changed into my sleeping robe, crawled in under the mosquito netting, pushed the red blanket aside, flopped down onto the bedding backside first with an emphatic thud, and lay there on my back. This is the same way I've been getting into bed ever since I was little. Once when I was living in that boardinghouse in Tokyo the law student who was in the room underneath mine came up to complain about it, saying it was a bad habit. Even

though law students are weaklings they do have big mouths,
and this one started to deliver a long, nonsensical speech so I
shut him up by telling him that if he heard a lot of noise when
I went to bed it wasn't my backside's fault, it was because the
building was so flimsy, and if he had a problem he should take
it up with the owners. Since this night duty room wasn't on the
second floor, though, I could make as much noise as I wanted
when I dropped onto the bedding and it wouldn't bother anybody. If I can't do it with a nice, big crash, I just don't feel
like I'm really going to sleep. But just as I was stretching out and
starting to feel really comfortable, I felt something land on my
legs. Whatever it was had a rough, scratchy feel to it, so I knew
it couldn't be fleas. Feeling a little rattled, I shouted 'What the
. . . ?!' and tried shaking my legs a couple of times under the
blanket. As soon as I did this, I could feel more of the scratchy
things all over me – on five or six places on my shins, two or
three on my thighs, one that I squashed with my behind, one
that even jumped right up onto my belly button – now I was
really rattled! I bolted straight out of bed, yanked the blanket
down, and saw a swarm of fifty or sixty grasshoppers leaping
up off the mattress. Until I realized what was going on the whole
thing had felt pretty creepy, but once I figured out what I was
dealing with I got really mad. If you think a bunch of grasshoppers is enough to put a scare into somebody, just you get a load
of this, I thought, and I grabbed my pillow and started bashing
away at them, but they made such small targets that no matter
how hard I swung it I didn't accomplish much. For lack of a
better strategy, I sat back down on the mattress and began swat-
ting at it wildly in all directions, the way you might do when
you're trying to beat the dust out of a floor mat. The force of
my attack made the startled grasshoppers leap even higher – they
were crashing into my shoulders, my head, some even latched
onto the tip of my nose. I couldn't get rid of the ones that were
sticking to my face by whacking them with the pillow, so I picked
them off and flung them away as hard as I could. No matter
how hard I threw the damned things, there was nothing to show
for it but a gentle ripple on the mosquito netting when they hit
it. They stayed perched on the netting right where they landed.

They wouldn't die; they wouldn't do anything. After about thirty minutes of this I finally managed to get rid of them all. Then I went and got a broom and started sweeping up all the dead ones. At this point the custodian came in and asked what had happened. 'What do you mean, what happened?' I shouted. 'Did you ever hear of a place where people keep grasshoppers in their bed, you idiot?' 'I wouldn't know, sir,' he answered apologetically. 'Is that the best you can say for yourself?' I said, flinging the broom out onto the veranda. He beat a hasty retreat with the broom on his shoulder and an embarrassed look on his face.

I immediately called for three of the boarding students to come out as representatives of the whole group. Instead, six of them turned up. Six, ten, whatever, it didn't make a bit of difference to me. Still in my night robe, I rolled up my sleeves and began the interrogation.

'Why the devil did you put those grasshoppers in my bed?'

'Uhh, grasshoppers? What do you mean?' said the one standing at the front of the group. This was way too casual. It wasn't just the Principal who tried to beat around the bush at this school; the students had the same way of talking.

'You don't know what a grasshopper is? Well, look at this!' I yelled, but unfortunately they'd all been swept up and there wasn't one to be seen. I called the custodian in and ordered him to bring some back, at which point he said 'I've already thrown them in the garbage, would you like me to pull them out?' 'Yes, do it right now,' I said, and he scurried off. Before long he was back with about a dozen of them piled on a piece of writing paper: 'So sorry, sir, but what with it being nighttime and all, these were all I could find. I'll bring some more tomorrow morning.' What a fool! I took one of the insects, held it up in front of the students, and said 'This is a grasshopper – see how big they are? Now, don't tell me you don't know what they are!' 'No,' said a moon-faced boy on the left edge of the group, 'that's a locust, na moshi.' The kid had some nerve, but now *I* was on the spot. 'Grasshoppers, locusts, they're all the same! And who do you damned jackasses think you are sticking that stupid na moshi on the end of everything when you're talking to a teacher? It just makes you sound mushy – that's all it's good for!' That ought to show them who's boss, I thought – but they came right back with 'Na moshi isn't the same as mushy – na moshi.' It was hopeless – they couldn't stop saying na moshi even if they tried.

'Locusts, grasshoppers, whatever – what were you doing putting them in my bed? When did I ever tell you to do that?'

'Nobody put them there.'

'Oh yeah? So what were they doing there?'

'Well, locusts like warm places, so they must have decided to go in there on their own . . .'

'What kind of nonsense is that? A bunch of grasshoppers decided to go in there on their own? Do you think I'm going to stand for this? Just tell me why you pulled a stunt like that – come on!'

'There's nothing to tell. How can we tell you anything if we didn't do it?'

How shabby could you get? If you're not going to own up to what you've done, you shouldn't have done anything in the first place. They obviously figured that as long as no evidence turned up, all they had to do was play dumb and they'd get away with it – of all the nerve! Of course, I'd been involved in my share of pranks myself when I was in middle school, but when they asked me whether I was the one who did it, I would never, ever try to weasel out of it. If I did it, I did it, and if I didn't, I didn't; that's all there was to it. No matter how much mischief I was involved in, I still had my honor. If you're just going to lie your way out of the punishment afterward, well, you shouldn't have done anything to begin with. Mischief and punishment go hand in hand – it's knowing that the punishment comes with it that makes it fun to dare to do the mischief. Did they really think that there was some low-down country out there where people could play tricks and then claim immunity from the consequences? This must be the way that those characters who borrow money off you and then refuse to pay it back get their start in life, too. Just what were these kids doing in a middle school anyway? If they thought that getting an education is about learning to lie and fake and play mean tricks when nobody's looking, and then parading around proudly when you graduate, they still had a lot to learn. What riffraff!

Getting into a debate with a bunch of kids who had such a rotten attitude made me feel sick to my stomach, so I just said 'All right, never mind. If you're in middle school and you still don't know anything about what it means to have some class, you're pathetic,' and sent all six of them back to bed. There may be nothing very classy about the way I talk or the way I look, but I think I can say that when it comes to heart the quality is there, which is a lot more than you could say for them. The six of them drifted away, looking so cool and composed that if you were only judging by appearances, you could say that they cut much finer figures than I, their teacher, did. But in fact their attitude just showed all the more clearly how little class they really had. I could never pull off anything like that myself.

Finally I was able to stretch out in bed again, but in all the commotion the mosquitoes had made their way inside the netting and now they were buzzing around all over the place. It would have been way too hard to try to get rid of them by burning them one at a time with my candle, so I took down the netting, folded it lengthwise on the floor, and shook it out from each side. While I was doing this, one of the metal fastening rings smacked the back of my hand so hard it made me groan. Back in bed for the third time, I finally started to calm down a little, but I still couldn't get to sleep. The clock said half past ten. I lay there thinking about what a mess I had gotten myself into by coming here. If being a middle school teacher meant that you had to put up with kids like these no matter where you went, it was pretty sad. It was a wonder they didn't run out of teachers. I guess it's a job for people who are tremendously patient, and thick-skulled as well. It was certainly more than I could take. When you think about it, you really have to hand it to somebody like Kiyo. She was just an old woman without any education or social standing, but as a human being she was really noble. Even though she'd done so much for me, I'd never felt particularly grateful to her before, but now that I found myself on my own so far away from home I finally realized how kindhearted she'd been. If she wanted some of those sweets from Echigo, it would certainly be worth making a trip there just to get some for her. She used to praise me for having an unselfish, upstanding character, but if anybody was

going to be praised for being a truly fine person, she deserved it
a lot more than I did. How I longed to see her then!

As I lay there tossing and turning with these thoughts of Kiyo
running through my mind, all of a sudden I heard the sound of
what must have been thirty or forty pairs of feet pounding stead-
ily on the wooden floor directly above my head, so hard that it
seemed like the ceiling might come crashing down on me any
minute. Then they started yelling at a volume that matched the
stamping. I bolted out of bed again, wondering what could possibly be going on. As soon as I was up I realized it had to be the
students, trying to get back at me . . . You guys, I thought to
myself . . . Until you acknowledge that what you did was wrong,
you're still guilty in my eyes. You must have realized it was
wrong. The decent thing to do would be to go back to your beds
and think it over and, once you've had some second thoughts,
come and apologize in the morning. Or even if you couldn't
bring yourselves to do that, the least you could do would be to
feel a little ashamed of yourselves and go to sleep quietly. And
instead you go in for more mayhem? Don't you know that this
is supposed to be a dormitory, not a pigpen? You'd better cut
back on these crazy stunts. Just you wait . . . I dashed out of my
room, still in my night robe, and bounded up the stairway to
the second floor. To my amazement the racket that had been
erupting just above my head had suddenly turned into absolute
silence; not a hint of those screaming voices, let alone pounding
feet. Very strange! The lamps were already out so it was too dark
to see anything clearly, but I could sense that some of them were
lurking here and there. But there was nobody, not even a mouse,
in the hallway that ran the length of the dormitory from east to
west. Down at the far end there was a bright patch where the
moon was shining in. Definitely strange, like the times years ago
when I used to have all kinds of dreams and then wake up with
a jolt and start babbling a stream of nonsense. I used to get
laughed at a lot for that. Once when I was sixteen or seventeen
I even had this dream about finding a diamond and I sprang out
of bed and furiously asked my brother, who was lying next to
me, where my diamond was. The whole household wouldn't
stop laughing at me for three days, which was very hard to take.

For all I knew, what was happening now might be a dream, too. But I *had* heard them carrying on . . .

As I stood there sunk in my thoughts, the silence was suddenly shattered by dozens of voices screaming 'One, two, three . . . YAAAAAHHH!!!' from down at the end of the corridor where the moon was shining in so brightly, followed in no time by the same rhythmic stomping of feet on the wooden floor that I'd heard before. So it hadn't been a dream after all. 'QUIET!! It's the middle of the night!!' I roared in a voice loud enough to make myself heard over the racket, and I started to run down toward the far end of the hallway. Since it was dark all around me, all I could do was head for that patch of moonlight at the end. I had only gone a couple of yards when my shins banged into something hard right in the middle of the corridor, and before I could even hear myself yelling 'OW!!' I was dropping to the floor with a resounding crash. Damn them, I thought as I pulled myself back up, but no matter how hard I tried I couldn't run any more; my leg just refused to do what it was told. Seething, I hopped down to the end on my good foot, but by then the stomping and the shouting had turned to silence again and everything was still. No matter how low human beings sink, it's not possible for them to sink this low. These kids really were more like pigs than humans. If this is the way they want it, I decided, I wasn't going to leave until I had dragged them out of their hiding places and made them apologize, no matter how long it took, but when I tried to push open the door to get into one of their rooms it wouldn't budge. I couldn't tell whether they had locked it or shoved some desks or other furniture against it; either way, I couldn't get it to open however hard I pushed. I tried the door across the corridor. It didn't budge any more than the first one did. While I furiously kept trying to push my way into the room and grab one of the kids, the jeering and stomping started up all over again at the other end of the hallway.

Finally I realized what was going on: the little devils had it all planned out so they could give it to me from both sides. But what could I do about it? I'll have to admit it: I may have courage, but I don't have the brains to match. When I get myself into

this kind of fix, I'm totally at a loss. But even if I'm at a loss, I'll
be damned if I'm going to be a loser. To give up at this point
would have been a disgrace. It would have been awful to let
them have an excuse for claiming that Tokyo people have no
guts. If people were to hear that I allowed this pack of snot-nosed
brats to make a fool out of me while I was on duty and simply
slunk back to my room because I couldn't handle them, I would
never live it down. Whatever faults I may have, my ancestors
were retainers of the Shogun, a line of warriors going back to
the Emperor Seiwa and descended from the great Minamoto no
Mitsunaka. I'm not made of the same stuff as those peasants
were, of that you can be sure. If only I could think of something!
If only there was some way out of this mess! Anyhow, I wasn't
about to give in. Being honest, I couldn't see a way out. But after
all, if you can't win with honesty, what else is there? All right, I
decided, if I couldn't win tonight, I'd win tomorrow. If I couldn't
win tomorrow, I'd win the day after. And if I couldn't win the
day after, I'd just have my meals delivered from home and stay
right where I was until I did win. I sat myself down right in the
middle of the corridor, ready to wait there until the morning.
The mosquitoes were buzzing all around me, but I didn't care.
When I rubbed the spot on my shin I had banged before, I could
feel something wet and sticky. It must have been bleeding. Fine,
let it bleed if it wanted to. Finally fatigue started to catch up
with me and I fell asleep. But then my sleep was broken off by
some kind of commotion, and I pulled myself up with a curse.
The door to my right was half open, and two boys were standing there in front of me. As soon as I'd come to my senses I
grabbed one of the legs of the kid closest to me and jerked it
toward me as hard as I could. He came crashing down flat on
his back. That'll show you! Then I jumped the other one, who
was still just standing there in a kind of daze, grabbed him by
the shoulders, and gave him a good shaking up. He was so
stunned that all he could do was keep standing there and blink-
ing his eyes. When I said 'All right, you two, come with me,' and
bundled them off to my room, they both came along meekly,
like the sissies I took them for. By this time morning had already
broken.

When we got back to the night duty room I began my interrogation, but no matter how hard you beat it a pig is still a pig,
and the only thing I could get out of them was 'Uhh, I don't
know'; they weren't about to confess to anything. By and by the
rest of the students started coming downstairs in ones and twos
and gathering in front of my room. They all looked sleepy, with
puffy eyes. Shabbier than ever! How could you call yourself a
man if you ended up with a face like that after nothing worse
than losing a night's sleep? I told them to go get their faces
washed and then we would talk, but none of them left.

After I had spent the better part of an hour going back and
forth with all fifty-something of them and getting nowhere, the
Badger suddenly turned up. As I found out later, the custodian
had gone to his house to report that there was some kind of
commotion going on at school. The fact that he would go to the
bother of calling on the Principal over an incident like this just
shows what a faint-hearted type he was. No wonder he ended
up as a school custodian!

I gave the Principal a general account of what had happened,
and then he listened to a little of what the students had to say
for themselves. He announced that he would take appropriate
measures later, but meanwhile they should continue with their
studies as usual. Then, after telling them to hurry up and get
washed and have their breakfast because they'd be late for class
if they didn't get moving, he let them all go. This was being much
too easy on them. If it had been up to me, I would have expelled
them all on the spot. If they were going to be treated so leniently,
why shouldn't they harass a night duty teacher? Next the Principal turned to me and said that since I must be quite worn out
from the strain, I would be excused from offering instruction
today, to which I replied 'No, sir, it was no strain at all. Even if
this were to happen every night, I would never feel any strain
over it for as long as I live. I will teach my classes. If I was ever
unable to teach simply because of losing a night's sleep, I'd return
that portion of my salary to the school.' The Principal just gazed
at me for a couple of moments with an inscrutable expression;
then he said 'But your face looks quite swollen, you know.' It was
true, it did feel kind of heavy and a little numb. It was itching all

over, too; the mosquitoes must have really worked it over. 'No matter how swollen my face is, my mouth is still working fine,' I said, scratching away at it all the while. 'There won't be any problems with today's classes.' 'Quite a sturdy fellow, aren't you?' he said with a laugh. This wasn't really supposed to be a compliment, I think; it sounded kind of snide.

5

'How would you like to do a little fishing?' Redshirt asked me.

His tone of voice was so gentle that it made you feel creepy. You could hardly tell whether it was a man's voice or a woman's. If you're a man, you should talk like one – all the more so if you're a university graduate. If somebody like me, who only went to the Institute of Physical Sciences, can have the kind of voice I do, it was really a disgrace for a man with a university degree to talk the way he did.

'Well, I guess so,' I answered, without very much enthusiasm, at which point he was rude enough to ask me if I had ever gone fishing before. It's true that I haven't done much, but I did catch three silver carp once when I was a kid at a fishing hole in Komume. I also hooked an eight-inch carp once at the Bishamon festival in Kagurazaka, but when I tried to pull it out it dropped back into the water with a big splash; it still bothers me to think that I let it get away like that. When I told all this to Redshirt, he just stuck out his chin and laughed that effeminate laugh of his. I didn't see what was so funny.

'Well, then, you haven't experienced the joys of fishing yet, have you? I'd be glad to initiate you if you like,' he said in an extremely smug tone. Who did he think would want his initiation? To begin with, fishermen and hunters are downright inhumane in my opinion. If they weren't, there's no way that they'd get any pleasure out of killing living things. Anybody can see that a fish or a bird would rather be alive than be killed. If you have to fish or hunt in order to make your living that's a different story, but if you're not lacking for anything and you still can't get to sleep at night unless you've gone out and killed some living creature, that's going too far. These were the thoughts that were running through my head, but of course I don't have the way with words a university man does, so instead of getting into a debate with him I just kept them all to myself. He must have thought that he had won me over by now, and kept right after me, saying 'Let's start the initiation right away. How about going out today, if you've got the time? It'll be more fun that way for Yoshikawa and me too, so please come along.'

Yoshikawa was the art teacher, the one I'd given the nickname the Hanger-on. For some reason he was always hanging around at Redshirt's place, and he'd tag along after Redshirt wherever he went, as if he were some kind of personal attendant instead of a colleague. I knew that if Redshirt was going somewhere the Hanger-on was bound to be there too, so it wasn't any surprise that they were going fishing together, but why did they have to invite an unsociable guy like me along instead of just enjoying it by themselves? I guessed that they must have wanted to show off this elegant pastime of theirs. As if I was the type to be impressed! Even if they managed to land a couple of tuna somehow, did they really think I would give a damn? Anyway, beginner or not, I was just as much of a man as they were, so I'd probably manage to catch something. And besides, knowing Redshirt, he'd probably think that if I didn't go it must be because I'm a lousy fisherman, not because I wasn't interested. So, finally, I told him I'd go. After school, I went home and got ready, then I went to the station to meet the other two, and we headed down to the harbor. There was just one boatman, with a long, narrow boat that didn't look like any I'd ever seen in the waters around Tokyo. There were no fishing poles in sight. I had no idea how we were supposed to catch fish without a pole, but when I asked the Hanger about it he simply stroked his chin and explained, as if he was some kind of expert, that you don't use a pole to fish offshore, you just use a line. If this was the kind of put-down I was going to get, I would have been better off just keeping my mouth shut.

The boatman kept plying his oar in the same slow, easy rhythm, but there's nothing like a professional: by the time I glanced back at the harbor, we were already so far out that it

was starting to look pretty small. The slender pagoda of Kōhaku
Temple rose up out of a grove of trees like a needle. On the other
side of the boat we could see Green Island floating on the water.
This island, I was told, was uninhabited. When you looked
closely you could see that it was nothing but boulders and pine
trees – no wonder nobody lived there. Redshirt surveyed the
scene intently and announced that it was quite beautiful. The
Hanger agreed that it was absolutely superb. I wasn't sure how
superb it was, but I was certainly feeling pretty good. Just being
out on that broad expanse of water with a cool sea breeze blow-
ing would be a pleasure for anybody. I was getting really hungry.

'Now look at that pine tree – the one with the straight trunk
and the top opening out like an umbrella – it's like something
out of a Turner painting,' Redshirt said. 'Yes, yes, just like a
Turner – look at the way it curves, it's just right – it *has* to be a
Turner,' said the Hanger, looking pleased with himself. I had no
idea what a Turner was, but it didn't seem to be worth asking
about, so I just kept quiet.

The boat swung around to the left of the island. There wasn't
a wave to be seen. It was so calm that you would hardly even
think you were out on the sea. Thanks to Redshirt, I was really
enjoying myself. I was thinking that we should try putting in at
the island, but when I asked them if we could land by one of the
rocks, Redshirt said it wasn't impossible but the fishing wouldn't
be good if we went in too close. I didn't reply. Then the Hanger
broke in with a totally inane question: 'What do you think, sir,
from now on shouldn't we call it Turner Island?' Redshirt agreed
that it was a fine idea. Count me out, I thought to myself; Green
Island was just fine with me. The Hanger's next suggestion was
that it would make a good picture if we could set Raphael's
Madonna up on that rock, but this time Redshirt's answer was
'Let's not talk about Madonnas,' with one of those mild-mannered,
creepy laughs of his. He looked distinctly uncomfortable. The
Hanger said there was nothing to worry about since there was
nobody around to overhear, but then he glanced over in my
direction and lowered his gaze with a silly smirk. I was beginning
to feel a little on edge myself. Madonnas, prima donnas, whatever – it didn't have anything to do with me, so they could stick

anybody they wanted up there as far as I was concerned. But talking about things that other people don't understand, and acting like it doesn't matter if they overhear you precisely because they won't understand, is downright tacky. And to think that the Hanger called himself a native Tokyo man! I figured that this Madonna they were talking about must be their nickname for some geisha that Redshirt was seeing. If he wanted to stand his favorite geisha under a pine tree on a deserted island and enjoy the scene, that was okay with me. And if the Hanger wanted to paint her portrait in oils and show it at an exhibition somewhere, well, let him!

The boatman said that we were at a good spot and threw the anchor overboard. When Redshirt asked how deep the water was, he said about six fathoms. Redshirt said that it was pretty hard to fathom how we were going to find any bream at that depth and flung his line into the water. So the big boss was after a bream, was he? Very intrepid! But the Hanger said that Redshirt, being the expert fisherman that he was, was sure to land one, especially with the water being so calm, and accompanied this bit of flattery with a cast of his own line. To my surprise, the lines only had lead sinkers on the end. No floats. Trying to fish without a float is kind of like trying to take somebody's temperature without a thermometer. I couldn't see any point to it, but Redshirt said 'Come on now, try it yourself. Have you got a line?' I told him that I had plenty of line but no float, to which he replied that floats were only for amateurs. When your line hits bottom, he explained, you just hold it down against the gunwale with your index finger and feel for a tug, like this – look, there's one now! Redshirt started reeling in his line right away, as if he was sure he had caught something, but all he came up with was a bare hook with the bait gone. Served him right!

'Ah, what a shame!' said the Hanger. 'It certainly must have been a big one. Now, if it was able to get away from an expert like you, sir, we'll all really have to be on our toes today. But even so, it still beats sitting there just staring at your float like the beginners do, doesn't it? Why, they're no better than those people who can't ride a bicycle without brakes.' Listening to him spout this nonsense, I was just itching to treat him to a good beating. I mean, I'm a man, too, and it wasn't as if the Assistant Principal had rented out the entire sea for his own personal use – it was big enough for all of us! Thinking that a nice juicy bonito really ought to come along and at least take a nibble at my line, if only as a matter of principle, I threw it into the water with a satisfying splash and wiggled it lazily with my fingertip.

By and by, I began to feel something pulling on the line. It had to be a fish, I thought to myself. Anything that could tug that hard would have to be alive. Gotcha! I started hauling it in as fast as I could. 'Oh my, did you catch something? A classic case of beginner's luck,' said the Hanger in a mocking tone. I had pulled my line almost all the way back in; there were only a couple of feet left in the water. Peering over the side, I saw that what I had hooked was a striped fish that looked something like a goldfish. It was lunging this way and that as I hauled it up. Now this was fun! When I pulled it to the surface, it broke the water with splash, drenching my face into the bargain. Finally I managed to grab the thing and tried to take the hook out of its mouth, but this turned out to be no easy trick. It felt all slimy in my hand – yuck!! I just gave up and flung it down onto the floor of the boat, line and all, and it died almost immediately. Redshirt and the Hanger were watching all this with amazement. I scrubbed my hands with some seawater and took a sniff. They still had a fishy smell. I had learned my lesson: no matter what I caught, I wanted no part of holding it. The fish probably didn't want any part of it either. I wound up my line right away.

'Well, good for you, you've scored the first point, but it's only a *goruki*,' said the Hanger, playing the smart aleck again, at which point Redshirt cracked a joke: 'Goruki? Sounds like he's hooked a Russian novelist.' Of course the Hanger had to chime in right away: 'Oh yes! Gorky, the Russian novelist. Very good!' All right, so a goruki is a Russian novelist, Maruki is a photographer's studio back in Tokyo, and a door key gets you into your house. Redshirt just loved dropping foreign names, making it sound like he was pronouncing them in some foreign alphabet, no matter who he was talking to. A totally obnoxious habit. Everyone has their own field of knowledge. How was a math teacher like me supposed to know the difference between Gorky and Porky? Better to give it up. If he was going to throw around this foreign stuff at all, he should have stuck with things that even people like me have heard of, like Benjamin Franklin's autobiography. Sometimes he would bring this magazine with a bright red cover called *Imperial Literature* to school with him and read it as if it was the greatest thing around. When I asked the Porcupine about it, he told me that that was where he got all those foreign names of his. As far as I was concerned, that magazine was his partner in crime!

Redshirt and the Hanger kept fishing away, and in the space of about an hour they managed to land fifteen or sixteen fish between them. The funny thing was, every last one of the fish they caught was a goruki. There wasn't even the slightest hint of a bream. 'It's a good day for Russian literature,' Redshirt said to the Hanger, who replied that if goruki were what an expert like Redshirt was catching, someone like himself certainly couldn't hope for anything else. According to the boatman, these fish are full of bones and have an awful taste, definitely not fit for eating; you could use them for fertilizer, though. So Redshirt and the Hanger had been busy fishing for fertilizer, then. It was absolutely pathetic. My one catch had been more than enough for me, and since then I had been lying on my back in the bottom of the boat and gazing up at the sky. This was a much more elegant pastime than fishing.

Before long the two of them began talking to each other about something in a hushed tone. I couldn't hear them very well, and didn't want to. As I gazed at the sky I was thinking about Kiyo. I was thinking how nice it would be if I had some money and I could bring her here to enjoy this pretty place. No matter how splendid the scenery was, it was no fun being here with the likes of the Hanger. Kiyo might be a wrinkled old woman, but I wouldn't feel embarrassed to take her anywhere. People like the Hanger weren't worth associating with no matter where you were – in a carriage, on a boat, even at the top of the twelve-story tower in Asakusa Park back in Tokyo. I was sure that if I were the Assistant Principal and Redshirt were in my position, I'd be the one this guy was buttering up and flattering all over the place, and Redshirt would be the one he was always sneering at. They say that Tokyo people are two-faced, and now I was beginning to see why: if a guy like the Hanger was going around the country telling everybody about how he was a true son of Tokyo at every chance he got, it's no wonder that country people thought that 'two-faced' was just another way of calling somebody a Tokyoite, and vice versa.

As these thoughts were passing through my head, I could hear the two of them breaking into a kind of muffled giggle. In between the laughs they were saying something to each other, but I could only make out bits and pieces of it and couldn't catch the drift: 'What? Do you mean to say that . . .' '. . . It's awful . . . had absolutely no idea . . . such a disgrace . . .' 'How could? . . .' 'Yes, grasshoppers . . . it's the truth . . .'

I wasn't listening to any of this very carefully, but when I heard the word 'grasshoppers' coming out of the Hanger's mouth it jolted me to attention. For some reason he had put particular emphasis on it, as if to make sure that I would hear it loud and clear, but then he deliberately went back to that muffled tone. I kept still and went on listening.

'That Hotta's at it again . . .' 'Hmm, maybe so . . .' 'Tempura . . . hahahahaha . . .' '. . . and incited . . .' '. . . and dumplings, too? . . .'

These bits and pieces were all that I could catch, but judging from the words that I was able to make out – 'grasshoppers,' 'tempura,' 'dumplings' – they could only have been having a confidential talk about me. If they wanted to have a talk, they should have done it in a regular voice; if they had something confidential to discuss, well, they shouldn't have invited me along. What a pair of creeps! Grasshoppers, glass choppers, whatever it was, it hadn't been any fault of mine. That badger of a Principal had said that he would deal with the incident himself, so I was just going along and staying out of things for now. Just who did the Hanger think he was, sticking in his own totally uncalled-for comments like this? He should have stuck to sucking on his brushes and kept out of it. Anyway I knew that I would get around to settling my own accounts sooner or later, so I didn't care what they were saying about me, but things

like 'That Hotta again' and 'incited' did make me feel uneasy.
Did they mean that the Porcupine had incited me to turn the
incident into a big brouhaha? Or that he had incited the students
to go after me? I couldn't figure out what they were getting at.
As I kept gazing up into the blue, the sunlight was getting fainter
and fainter, and a slightly chilly breeze was starting to blow. Just
as the clouds, which had been as wispy as the smoke from an
incense burner, looked like they had quietly risen all the way up
into the clear depths of the heavens, I realized that they were
condensing into a faint mist.

'Well, shall we head back?' Redshirt asked, as if he'd just
thought of something. The Hanger said yes, it's the perfect time,
isn't it, and then asked Redshirt if he was planning to pay a call
on Mademoiselle Madonna that evening. Redshirt, who had
been leaning casually against the side of the boat, said 'Don't
say anything foolish, there could be trouble, you know,' and
pulled himself up a little. 'Hee hee, don't worry,' the Hanger
replied, 'even if he did hear . . .' When he quickly turned to look
at me, I gave him my best if-looks-could-kill glare, my eyes as
big as saucers. 'Uh-oh, that's too much for me!' he murmured,
looking for all the world as if he was blinded by my gaze, and
scratched his head as he tried to pull it in between his hunched-
up shoulders. What a charlatan!

The boatman rowed us back across the still waters to the
shoreline. When Redshirt said that it looked like I hadn't enjoyed
the fishing very much I agreed that I much preferred lying back
and looking up at the sky. I threw what was left of my cigarette
overboard; it hit the water with a hiss and then bobbed up and
down as it drifted on the current of the boatman's oar. Then,
suddenly, he changed the subject completely: 'The students are
so glad that you're here. We're counting on you to give it your
best effort.'

'They don't look very glad to me.'

'No, no, I'm not just saying this to make you feel good. They
really are glad. Aren't they, Yoshikawa?'

'They're more than glad, they're in an absolute frenzy,' said
the Hanger with that insinuating grin of his. It was amazing the
way every single thing he said got on my nerves somehow.

'But,' Redshirt added, 'if you aren't careful, you could get yourself into some real trouble.'

'I know it's out there. Whatever happens, I'll be ready for it.' In fact I was determined that I'd either get an apology from all the boarding students or get fired, one or the other.

'Well, if that's the way you feel about it there isn't much more I can say ... But I'm telling you this because as the Assistant Principal I only want what's best for you, and I hope you won't take it the wrong way.'

'That's right,' the Hanger chimed in. 'The Assistant Principal is completely on your side. And since you and I are both from Tokyo, I'm hoping that the two of us will be able to stick together for a good, long time. In my own little way I'm doing what I can on your behalf behind the scenes, you know.' For once, he was actually sounding like a regular guy. But I'd rather hang myself than feel beholden to the likes of him!

'Yes, the students are really happy that you've come to our school. But all the same, there are various circumstances that have to be taken into consideration. I know there may be times when you're going to get upset, but I hope that you'll just grin and bear it. And for my part, I'll never do anything that would end up hurting you.'

'"Various circumstances"? What do you mean?'

'Well, it's all a bit complicated, but you'll see it clearly enough for yourself by and by. Even without my explaining it, it will all become clear in due course. Won't it now, Yoshikawa?'

'Yes, yes, it *is* quite complicated, not the kind of thing that you can expect to understand overnight. But you'll see clearly enough for yourself by and by. Even without my explaining it, it will all become clear in due course.' These were virtually the same words that Redshirt had just used.

'Well, if it's that much of a bother I don't really need to hear about it, but since you were the one who mentioned it, I just thought I'd ask.'

'True enough. I was the one who brought it up, so it was a little irresponsible of me not to follow through. All right, then, let me just say this: pardon me for putting it this way, but you've only just received your diploma, and this is your first experience as a teacher. But there are all sorts of complicated personal considerations to take into account in a school, and it won't do to approach things as straightforwardly as you did when you were a student . . .'

'If it won't do to approach things straightforwardly, then what will?'

'Now, that's just what I'm trying to say: an inexperienced young man who speaks his mind the way you do still has a lot to learn . . .'

'Of course I'm inexperienced. I'm only twenty-two years and four months old, just like it says on my papers.'

'And that's why it would be so easy for someone to take advantage of you in ways you've never even dreamed of.'

'No matter what anybody tries to do to me, I won't have anything to be afraid of as long as I'm honest.'

'Of course you won't. Nothing to be afraid of – but they'll still take advantage of you. In fact, your own predecessor got taken in, and that's why I'm warning you to be on your guard.'

Suddenly I noticed that the Hanger had been keeping very quiet during all this. I looked around and saw that he had moved back to the stern of the boat and was talking fishing with the boatman. It was much easier for me to talk to Redshirt without him around.

'Who was it that took advantage of my predecessor?'

'I can't tell you who; we have to think about his reputation. Besides, we don't have all the evidence yet, so it wouldn't be right to reveal it now. At any rate, now that you're finally here, all of the work we put into bringing you here would go for nothing if something were to happen. Please be careful.'

'Yes, but I don't know how I can be any more careful than I am now. As long as I don't do anything wrong myself I'll be all right, won't I?'

Redshirt just laughed. I hadn't noticed that there was anything particularly funny about what I'd said. Right up to that point I'd always firmly believed that this was the way things should be. Now that I thought about it, though, I realized that most people actually encourage you to turn bad. They seem to think that if you don't, you'll never get anywhere in the world. And then on those rare occasions when they encounter somebody who's honest and pure-hearted, they look down on him and say he's nothing but a kid, a Botchan. If that's the way it is, it would be better if they didn't have those ethics classes in elementary school and middle school where the teacher is always telling you to be honest and not to lie. The schools might as well just go ahead and teach you how to tell lies, how to mistrust everybody, and how to take advantage of people. Wouldn't their students, and the world at large, be better off that way? Redshirt had laughed at me for being simpleminded. If people are going to get laughed at for being simpleminded and sincere, there's no hope. Kiyo never laughed at me for saying anything like what I said to Redshirt. She would have been deeply impressed by it. Compared to Redshirt, she's far and away the superior person.

'Of course you'll be all right if you don't do anything wrong, but even if you don't do anything wrong yourself, you could get into some serious trouble if you don't realize how wrong other people can be. You may meet some people who seem nice and easygoing, or who seem to be totally aboveboard, or who even go out of their way to help you find a place to live, but I'd keep a pretty close eye on them if I were you . . . Hmm, getting a bit chilly, isn't it? Well, it must be autumn, there's that sepia tint in the mist along the shore. What a view!' Now Redshirt turned toward the Hanger and shouted 'Hey, Yoshikawa! How about that view of the shore – really something, isn't it?' 'Yes indeed, absolutely splendid. If there was time I could have done a sketch. What a shame!' the Hanger replied, not missing the chance to play up to Redshirt yet again.

Just as a lamp was being lit on the second floor of the harbor inn and a train whistle came pealing through the air, the prow of our boat slid up onto the sand and came to a stop. The proprietress of the inn, standing on the shore, welcomed Redshirt back. I leapt over the side of the boat onto the beach, letting loose with a loud yell as I did so.

6

I couldn't stand the Hanger-on. If somebody tied him to a nice big rock and dumped him in the ocean, they'd be doing Japan a favor. The sound of Redshirt's voice made me sick. He could only get it to sound so smooth by using that stuck-up tone instead of his natural voice. No matter how stuck-up he sounded, though, it could never work with a face like that. If anybody was going to fall for it, it could only be somebody like the Madonna. Anyway, since he was the Assistant Principal, it was no wonder that what he said was harder to figure out than what the Hanger said. After I went home and did some thinking about what he'd told me, I came to the conclusion that there might well have been something to it. Since he didn't spell everything out clearly, I couldn't be completely sure that I understood what he was getting at, but basically the point seemed to be that the Porcupine was a bad guy and that I had better watch out for him. If that was it, though, he should have come right out and said so like a real man. And if the Porcupine was really such a bad teacher, he ought to just go ahead and fire the guy right away. For somebody who had a university degree the Assistant Principal was surprisingly fainthearted. He had to be a real weakling if he couldn't even bring himself to name names when he was talking behind people's backs. Weaklings are usually kindhearted people, so you might expect Redshirt to be kind too, in that womanish way of his. Kindness is one thing and a voice is another, so it would have been wrong not to take his kindness for what it was just because I didn't care for his voice. Still, the world is a strange place when you think about it: a guy who rubs you the wrong way treats you kindly while a friend, somebody you get along with fine, turns out to be a scoundrel; it all seems like some kind of farce. This being the country, I figured, everything must be the opposite of what it was in Tokyo. You've got to watch out in a place like this – for all I knew fire might suddenly turn to ice out here, or the rocks might turn into lumps of tofu. But even so, the Porcupine stirring up the students against me? He hardly seemed to be the type for that kind of mischief . . . but then again . . . He was supposed to be the most popular teacher, so maybe he would be able to get away with just about anything he wanted, and yet . . . In the first place, if he were to just come after me in person and pick a fight, it certainly would have been a lot less trouble than taking such a roundabout approach. You would think that if he had some kind of problem with me, all he had to do was come and tell me what it was and demand that I resign. You can always work these things out if you talk them over. If it turned out that he was right, I'd be ready to hand in my resignation as of the following day. It wasn't as if this was the only job in the world. No matter where I ended up, I was sure I'd manage to keep from starving. This Porcupine, I thought, could have used a little more sense.

The Porcupine had been the first to treat me to a dish of shaved ice after I got here. But to let myself be treated to anything by such a two-faced guy, even just a dish of ice, would be a disgrace. All I had was one helping, so it only cost him one and a half sen. But to be beholden to such a phony, even just a sen's or even a half sen's worth, would make me feel awful for the rest of my life. Tomorrow, I decided, I'd return the money as soon as I got to school. Now, there were also those three yen I had borrowed from Kiyo five years ago, which I had never paid back. It wasn't that I didn't have the money; I simply hadn't done it. Nor, of course, did she have any expectation that I'd be paying her back any time either. And I, for my part, had no intention of repaying her as if it was just some financial transaction between two strangers. If I was to treat it that way, it would seem as if I didn't really believe in Kiyo's generosity, as if I was denying the purity of her feelings for me. The reason I hadn't returned it wasn't because I was trying to cheat her; it was because I thought of her as part of my own self. Of course there was a world of difference between Kiyo and the Porcupine, but when somebody treats you to something and you make no effort to decline it, whether it's a dish of shaved ice, a cup of sweet tea, or whatever, well, it shows the kind of respect and goodwill you have for that person. The sense of gratitude that you feel in your heart when you accept a favor from someone, which you could easily have avoided by paying your own way, is a form of giving back that goes beyond anything that money could buy. I may not have the kind of title or position that will impress people, but I'm still a free, full-grown human being. And when such a person finds you worthy of respect, you should consider it something more precious than a fortune in gold.

And yet, I felt, here I had let the Porcupine spend that sen and a half on me, and in return I had let him have that thing more precious than a fortune in gold. He certainly should have felt grateful, but instead he was engaging in underhanded schemes behind my back – it was disgusting! Tomorrow I'd go and return the money to him, and then neither of us would owe the other a thing. Once that was settled, I'd be ready to take him on.

Having figured that much out, I began to feel drowsy and soon dropped into a deep sleep. The next day I headed to school earlier than usual in order to carry out my plan and waited for the Porcupine to arrive, but there was no sign of him. The Pale Squash arrived; the Chinese classics teacher arrived; the Hanger-on arrived; even by the time Redshirt arrived the Porcupine's desk was still undisturbed, with just a single stick of chalk reposing on top in its holder. I had the coins stuck in my fist from the time I left home, the same way I would if I were on my way to the bathhouse, ready to hand back to him as soon as he walked in. When I finally opened my hand, they were coated with the sweat from my palm. Since he would probably make some kind of comment if I handed them over all greasy with sweat, I laid them on top of my desk, puffed on them until they were dry, and stuck them back in my hand. At this point Redshirt came over and started to apologize for what had gone on yesterday, saying that it must have been a hard day for me.

Not at all, I said; thanks to them, in fact, I had managed to work up a good appetite. Then, resting an elbow on the Porcupine's desk, he leaned his broad, flat face right up alongside my nose. Just as I was trying to figure out what he was up to, he asked me to keep what he and the Hanger had said yesterday when we were coming back in the boat strictly confidential, and added that he certainly hoped that I hadn't mentioned it to anyone already. That feminine voice of his made him sound really nervous. Of course I hadn't said anything so far. But since I was definitely planning to – I still had the money ready, gripped tightly in my hand – I would be in a bind if he tried to keep me from talking.

This Redshirt was really something: first he gives me that riddle which was so easy to solve, even if he never came right out and mentioned the Porcupine by name, and now he tells me that there will be trouble if I do figure it out. Hardly the kind of responsible behavior that you'd expect from an Assistant Principal! What he should have been doing was to get himself ready to step right into the thick of things, on my side of course, once the blades started flashing in my battle with the Porcupine. That's the kind of attitude you would expect from a real Assistant Principal, and that's the kind of attitude that would have entitled him to wear that red shirt of his.

When I told him I hadn't said a thing to anybody so far but I did intend to have things out with the Porcupine when he arrived, Redshirt looked terribly upset: 'No. That would be wrong and it would lead to problems. As far as Mr Hotta is concerned, I don't recall saying anything specific to you. If you do something rash now, it will put me in a very difficult position. I assume that you didn't join our staff in order to be a trouble-maker.' All I could offer in reply to this strange bit of gibberish was that of course I realized that it wouldn't be good for the school if somebody on its payroll started stirring up trouble. Well then, he said, please just keep yesterday's discussion between us, and don't mention it to anybody. By this point he had broken into a sweat. All right, I agreed, this won't be easy for me either, but if it's going to create such a problem for you, I won't do it. 'So I can count on you, then?' he asked insistently. It was hard to tell how far beyond skin deep that soft, feminine manner of his went. If all college graduates were like this, they didn't amount to much. He didn't seem to have the slightest idea how little sense he was making, how illogical he sounded with these requests of his – and yet he still couldn't bring himself to take me at my word? If nothing else, I'm a man. How could I ever go so low as to turn my back on someone and break a commitment I had made?

At this point the two teachers whose desks were on either side of mine arrived, so Redshirt beat a hasty retreat back to his own desk. Even his way of walking looked like an act: when he moved across the room he would take care to tread so lightly that he didn't make a sound. It had never occurred to me before that walking silently might be something to feel proud of; unless you're training to be a cat burglar, you might as well just do it in the ordinary way! When the bugle sounded for the first class, there was still no sign of the Porcupine. Since there was nothing else I could do, I simply left the money on my desk and went off to the classroom.

The class ended up running a little overtime, so by the time I got back to the faculty room all the other teachers were sitting at their desks and talking. The Porcupine had finally arrived, too; he was only late for work, not absent as I had guessed. As soon as he laid eyes on me, he announced that I was the one who was responsible for making him late, so I should be the one to pay his fine. I picked the coins up off my desk, put them down on his, and told him that I was paying him back for the shaved ice from the other day. 'What are you talking about?' he said with a laugh, but when he saw that I meant it he pushed the money back onto my desk and told me to stop playing stupid jokes. This was one porcupine, I realized, that was going to stand its ground.

'It's no joke, this is for real. There's no reason for me to be treated to any ices by the likes of you, so I'm paying you back. Why won't you take it?'

'Well, if some small change means that much to you I'll take it back, but how come it's so important to give it back all of a sudden, as if you just thought of it right now?'

'Right now, whenever – back it goes. I don't want you doing me any favors, so back it goes.'

The Porcupine gave me a cool stare and then a shrug. If I hadn't given my word to Redshirt I would have exposed his treachery and had it out with him right then and there, but since I was pledged to silence there was nothing I could do. Here I was turning deep red in the face and he was just shrugging it off – was this any way to behave?

'All right, I'll take the money. Now please pack up and get out of that place you're renting.'

'Just take it. Whether I want to get out of my place or not is my business, not yours.'

'Actually it isn't. Yesterday the landlord came to see me and told me that he wants you out, and when he explained why it sounded perfectly reasonable. But I figured that I'd better go and see for myself, just to make sure, so this morning I stopped by on the way to school and this time he told me everything.'

I didn't have a clue as to what he was talking about.

'How am I supposed to know what he told you? And who gave you the right to be the judge? If there's a problem, the first thing to do is talk it over. How dare you just assume that he must be right and then act so rudely with me?'

'All right, then, I'll tell you. Your manners are so awful the two of them don't know what to do with you. The lady of the house isn't there to be your personal servant, you know. Sticking your feet out and telling her to wipe them for you – it's simply outrageous!'

'Oh? And just when did I have her do that?'

'I really don't know if you did it or not, but anyway they've had it with you. They said they can make ten or fifteen yen any time they want by selling off a hanging scroll, so they don't need a lodger like you.'

'Those bare-faced liars! If they're so damned clever, why did they rent the room out to me in the first place?'

'How should I know? The point is that they did it, but now they're fed up with you and they want you out, so out you go!'

'Fine with me. Even if they begged me on their hands and knees I wouldn't stay there for anything. But don't you forget, it's all your fault for setting me up with those liars to begin with!'

'My fault? Are you sure it isn't just that you're one big pain in the neck?'

The Porcupine had just as much of a temper as I did, and he wasn't about to let me shout him down either. By this time everybody in the room was wondering what was going on and they were all watching us with their jaws hanging open. As far as I was concerned I hadn't done anything to be ashamed of, so I shot a glance around the whole room as I stood there. The only one who didn't look stunned was the Hanger-on, who was sitting there with an amused-looking smile. But as soon as I caught that squinty face of his full on with a menacing scowl that practically asked him if he was looking for trouble too, he meekly wiped off the smile and put on a more serious expression. He looked a little shaken. Before long the bugle sounded again, so the Porcupine and I broke off our confrontation and headed to class.

In the afternoon, there was a staff meeting to discuss what action to take regarding the disgraceful misconduct of the dormitory students the night before. It was the first time in my life that I'd been to a staff meeting so I had no idea what to expect, but I assumed that everybody would get together, each of the teachers would present his own opinion, and then the Principal would shape them into some kind of appropriate consensus. This is the way to handle things when you've got a problem that's hard to solve because the issues aren't clear-cut. But in a case like this, which anybody in his right mind would consider outrageous, holding a conference is just a waste of time. No matter who looked at it, no matter how, there was obviously only one conclusion you could draw. Since it was so clear-cut, the Principal should have just gone ahead and taken action right away. How indecisive could he be? If this was what it meant to be a Principal, then there really wasn't that much to it at all, and 'Principal' was just another way of saying 'Weak-kneed sluggard.'

The conference was held in a long, narrow room next to the Principal's office, which usually served as the faculty lunchroom. There were about twenty black leather chairs around a long table; it reminded me a little of one of those Western-style restaurants in the Kanda area back in Tokyo. At the head of the table sat the Principal, with Redshirt seated beside him. Everyone else was free to sit where they wanted, I was told, except that the physical education teacher always humbly took the seat at the foot of the table. Since I didn't know what to do, I seated myself between the science teacher and the Chinese classics teacher. Right across from me were the Porcupine and the Hanger-on. There were no two ways about it: the Hanger's face had 'low-grade' written all over it. The Porcupine's was far more impressive-looking, even if he was my enemy now. It made me think of a face that I'd seen in a painting at the Yōgen Temple in Kobinata at my father's funeral. The priest had explained that it was a picture of a Buddhist guardian god called Idaten. The Porcupine, still furious, was gazing wildly all around the room, his eyes gyrating in their sockets; when they landed on me, I glared right back – if he thought he was going to stare *me* down with that look, he'd have to think again – and rolled my eyes at him too for good measure. My eyes may not be much to look at, but when it comes to size, well, they're just as big as the next guy's, big enough, in fact, that Kiyo used to tell me I'd make a fine actor if I ever went on the Kabuki stage.

'Well, it appears that just about everyone is here,' the Principal began, at which point the school clerk, a man named Kawamura, did a head count. Somebody was missing. 'Short by one,' he reported, and tried to figure out who it was. There was nothing to figure out: the Pale Squash wasn't there. I don't know what kind of karmic connection there was between the two of us, but right from the first time I saw the man's face I hadn't been able to get it out of my mind. He was always the first one I noticed when I arrived in the faculty room, and even when I was just walking around somewhere his image would float into my mind's eye. When I went to the hot spring, I would sometimes find him sitting and soaking in the tub with that pale, puffy face of his. Whenever I said hello to him he would just mumble something back and bow so meekly that it made me feel sorry for him. Nobody in the whole school was as mild-mannered as the Pale Squash. He hardly ever smiled; he hardly ever said any more than he had to, either. 'Gentleman' was a word that I had come across sometimes in books, but I had always thought that even if it existed in the dictionary, there were no examples to be found in real life. When I met the Squash, though, I was so impressed that for the first time in my life I began to believe that maybe it was more than just a word after all.

Since the Squash had become such an important figure to me, it's no wonder that as soon as I walked into the meeting room I had noticed that he wasn't there. To tell the truth, I had even been planning to sit next to him, so I had discreetly been on the lookout for him as I came in. The Principal said that he would no doubt be turning up soon, opened the purple silk wrapping around a bundle of papers that was sitting on the table in front of him, and then looked over a document that seemed to be a mimeograph. Redshirt began rubbing his amber pipe with a silk handkerchief. This was one of his pastimes, just the kind of thing you'd expect from somebody like him. The others were whispering among themselves; the ones who needed something to do with their hands kept themselves busy tracing designs on the tabletop with the eraser ends of their pencils. The Hanger-on made a couple of attempts at striking up a conversation with the Porcupine, but all he got in return was a couple of grunts and ahhs: the Porcupine was obviously more interested in giving me the evil eye. I, still refusing to be outdone, glared right back.

Eventually the long-awaited Squash arrived, looking as pathetic as ever. He gave the Badger a ceremonious bow and apologized for being late, explaining that he had been unavoidably detained while attending to a certain matter. 'Well, then,' declared the Badger, 'I hereby call the meeting to order,' and had Kawamura, the clerk, pass out copies of the mimeograph. The first item on the agenda was 'Punishments'; then there was 'Control of Students,' followed by two or three other things. The Badger, in the stuffy tone he regularly adopted when presenting himself as the Spirit of Education personified, gave a speech that ran roughly as follows.

'All instances of inappropriate conduct occurring at this school, be they committed by students or by instructors, are manifestations of a lack of virtue on my part. Whenever such an incident is reported, the sense of shame that I endure compels me to look deep within myself and question my own worthiness as a Principal. Unfortunately, gentlemen, I must come before you once again to humbly offer my profound apologies on account of yet another such disturbance. However, as that which has been done cannot be undone, appropriate measures must now be taken. Since the facts of the matter are already known to you, I hereby request that you assist me by informing me, in a frank and open manner, of your thoughts as to how the situation may best be rectified.'

As I listened to these words, I thought to myself with admiration that beings such as Principals and badgers are indeed blessed with silver tongues. If the Principal was really assuming responsibility for the entire incident, and going so far as to speak of it as his own fault, a manifestation of his own lack of virtue, you would think that it would be better for him to forget about punishing the students and simply turn in his own resignation. In that case, there wouldn't have been any need to go to the bother of calling a staff meeting. All you needed was to use a little common sense. It was all perfectly clear: I had just been sitting there on night duty, and the students acted up. It wasn't my fault, it wasn't the Principal's; it was obviously theirs and theirs only. If the Porcupine had been involved in inciting them, then all you had to do was get rid of him along with the students. Who ever heard of somebody who makes it his business to cover other people's butts and then goes around proclaiming that those butts are actually his own? Nobody but a Badger could pull off that kind of trick. Having finished spouting these inane remarks, he looked around the room with a self-satisfied air. Nobody, however, had anything to say. The science teacher was gazing at a crow that was perched on the roof. The Chinese classics teacher was busy folding up his mimeographed sheet and then unfolding it again. The Porcupine was still glaring at me. If all conferences were such a farce, you'd be better off giving them a miss and taking a nap instead.

Since the silence was beginning to get to me I decided I would break it with a nice big speech of my own, but just as I was lifting my butt off the chair Redshirt started to say something, so

I stopped. He had put away his pipe, and as he talked he mopped his face with his striped silk handkerchief. This had to be something he'd managed to wheedle out of the Madonna; a man's handkerchief ought to be made of white linen. 'I, too,' he began, 'felt a sense of my own inadequacy as Assistant Principal when I heard about the misbehavior of the dormitory students, and I am deeply ashamed of my failure to provide proper moral guidance to these young people. Incidents of this sort are inevitably the result of some kind of shortcoming, and although this one may appear to be the fault of the students if we view it as an isolated episode, when we consider the fuller picture we may well find that in actuality the responsibility lies with the school. I believe, therefore, that treating what is merely a superficial phenomenon with severely punitive measures might in fact lead to negative consequences in the future. Furthermore, it is by no means impossible that what we have here is simply a spontaneous overflowing of youthful high spirits, and that the pranks in question were committed half-unconsciously, as it were, without consideration of right or wrong. Of course, any disciplinary action is entirely up to the discretion of the Principal, and I have no intention whatsoever of infringing on his prerogatives, but I do hope that allowances will be made and that the measures taken will be as lenient as possible.'

Just as the Badger had been acting like a Badger, Redshirt, I saw, was being Redshirt. Here he was, openly declaring that if the students ran wild it was not they themselves who were to blame, but the teachers. In other words, when a lunatic bashes somebody on the head it's the person being bashed that's the guilty party, and that's why the lunatic is bashing him. Thanks a lot! If the students find themselves suffering from an excess of youthful high spirits, let them go out to the schoolyard and try their hands at sumo. Did they really expect me to put up with them half-unconsciously sticking grasshoppers in my bed? At this rate, if you're murdered in your sleep Redshirt would probably be ready to claim that that was also done half-unconsciously and let the perpetrators go free.

As these thoughts were running through my mind I was thinking about getting up and saying something, but then again there wouldn't be any point in speaking up unless I could bowl them over with my eloquence. I have a habit of getting completely tongue-tied when I'm angry – after I get the first couple of words out I'm lost. Even though the Badger and Redshirt were no match for me when it came to character, both of them were certainly smooth talkers and it would be no fun if I gave them an opportunity to pick on me just because I couldn't express myself properly. I was sitting there trying to think of a way to put my thoughts into the right words when across the table from me the Hanger-on, of all people, suddenly stood up to speak. What made this clown think that his opinion was worth anything? 'The recent grasshopper incident and the ensuing commotion,' he intoned in that airy voice of his, 'are truly extraordinary events, sufficiently grave to compel all of us, as conscientious educators, to contemplate the future of our school with profound concern. At this juncture it is incumbent upon all of us, as educators, to devote ourselves wholeheartedly to careful reflection upon our own conduct, and to re-establish a firm sense of discipline in our school. The analyses that our Principal and Assistant Principal have just provided penetrate precisely to the core of the issue at hand and I endorse them without reservation. By all means, let the punishment be as lenient as possible.' These were fine-sounding remarks, but with no meaning, full of fancy Chinese-style phrases that I could barely make head or tail of. The only part I could make out clearly was the business about endorsing without reservation.

Even though I couldn't understand the point he was trying to make I was in an awful rage by now, and before I could even figure out what I was going to say I was on my feet. I got as far as 'I oppose without reservation . . .' but then I was at a loss. Finally I managed to add that 'I really can't stand such a preposterous course of action,' at which point everybody burst out laughing. 'The fault lies entirely with the students. If we don't make them apologize, they'll be doing this kind of thing all the time. Expelling them would not be going too far. The sheer impudence of it . . . just because they thought there was a new teacher . . .' After I sat down the science teacher, who was seated to my right, spoke up for the weak-kneed approach: 'It's true that the students are the ones who are to blame, but if we punish them too severely we could provoke a backlash which would just make things worse. I agree with the Assistant Principal that a lenient policy is best.' The Chinese classics teacher on my left also supported a policy of moderation. The history teacher said that he agreed with the Assistant Principal too. Damn it! Just about everybody was on Redshirt's side. If these characters wanted to get together and run a school, well, let them. As far as I was concerned, though, there were only two choices: either we would make the students apologize or I would resign. If Redshirt managed to carry the day, I was ready to go right home and start packing my bags. I knew that I didn't have enough eloquence at my command to convince this crew of anything, and even if I did, it wasn't as if I was looking forward to having anything further to do with them anyhow. If I wasn't going to be associated with the school any longer, why should I care what happened next? If I were to say anything else now they'd only start laughing again, that was for sure. So I just sat there, not bothering to speak out.

At this point the Porcupine, who had been listening in silence so far, sprang up out of his seat. I was sure that this guy would also declare his support for Redshirt, not that I gave a damn considering that he was my enemy anyway, but in a voice so powerful it seemed to rattle the windows, he said: 'I am absolutely opposed to the position taken by the Assistant Principal and the rest of you. That is to say, no matter how you consider the incident in question, there is no getting away from the fact that what we are dealing with here is a group of fifty dormitory students who engaged in a disrespectful attempt to take advantage of a certain newcomer to the teaching staff. The Assistant Principal seems to believe that the cause may be traced to the character of the teacher but, if you will excuse my saying so, I feel that he may have misstated the circumstances. This new teacher was assigned to night duty in the dormitory very shortly after his arrival here, less than twenty days after coming into contact with the students. A bare twenty days was not enough time to enable the students to develop a proper sense of his character as a man of learning. If he had been treated in such a disrespectful manner because he had proved himself unworthy of respect, there might indeed be reason to make allowances for the students' conduct, but to excuse the behavior of impudent students who would expose a new teacher to ridicule without cause would, in my opinion, call into question the good reputation of this school. The spirit of education involves more than the mere imparting of knowledge. Along with inculcating a noble, upright, and manly character, it also consists, I believe, in the elimination of undesirable traits such as vulgarity, superficiality, and arrogance. If we were to allow ourselves to temporize out of fear of a backlash or of exacerbating this disturbance, there would be no telling when we could ever rectify such negative tendencies. It is precisely to strive for the elimination of these tendencies that we serve at this school, and if we were to neglect this duty it would have been better, I believe, for us never to have become educators at all. For these reasons it is imperative, in my opinion, that we compel the entire body of dormitory students to offer a public expression of apology directly to the instructor in question.' Having said this, the Porcupine took his seat again with a thump. The entire room was speechless. Redshirt began rubbing his pipe again. I was tremendously happy. It was as if the Porcupine had said everything I had wanted to say for me. Being the simple kind of person I am, I had already completely forgotten how angry I'd been with him, and I glanced over in his direction with an expression of gratitude, but the look on his face was completely oblivious.

After a short while the Porcupine stood up again and made the following remarks: 'I would like to add one more point which I neglected to mention during my previous comments. It is my understanding that the instructor on dormitory duty on the night in question left his post to pay a visit to the hot spring. This, I believe, was totally inexcusable. For someone who had accepted the responsibility of standing watch over the school to take advantage of the situation and go off to bathe at a hot spring resort, of all places, simply because there was no one present to call him to account, is misconduct of a very serious kind. It is my hope that along with the disciplining of the students, the

Principal will immediately issue a stern reprimand to the party in question.'

He was a strange one, all right, this Porcupine: just when you thought he was praising you, he goes and points out your mistakes. Since I had seen how the night duty teacher had gone out for a walk on the night I arrived, I had assumed in all innocence that such things were allowed, and so I had gone off to the hot spring myself. Now that it was put to me this way, though, I could see that I'd been wrong. It was no wonder I was being criticized. With that I stood up and declared, 'It is indeed true that I went to the hot spring while on night duty. This was completely wrong. I apologize,' and sat back down, whereupon everybody burst out laughing again. It seemed like they were going to laugh every time I opened my mouth. What a worthless bunch! I'd like to see *them* try to stand up and openly admit that they had done something wrong – of course they couldn't, which is probably why they were laughing.

At that point the Principal announced that, as it appeared that everybody had now voiced their opinions, he would give them his full consideration before he took action. (What eventually happened, by the way, was that the dormitory students were confined to their quarters for a week, and they also offered me an apology, to my face. Considering how I had been prepared to hand in my resignation and go back home right then and there if they had not apologized, it actually might have been better if I hadn't gotten my way, since things ended up getting so messy anyway, but I'll explain about all that later.) The conference continued with the Principal offering the following comments: 'Because it is incumbent upon the faculty to exert a positive influence on the student body by setting a proper moral example, I would like to request, as a first step, that teachers refrain from patronizing public eating and drinking establishments. Of course, exceptions can be made in the case of farewell banquets and other such official functions, but I would ask that you refrain from dining alone in places that are not particularly reputable – places such as noodle shops, for instance, or dumpling shops . . .' As soon as he mentioned these, everyone was laughing again. The Hanger-on glanced over at the Porcupine and murmured 'tempura' with a knowing look, but the Porcupine just ignored him. Served him right!

Not being that bright, I had a pretty hard time following what the Badger was saying, but I was thinking to myself that if people who ate at places like noodle or dumpling shops couldn't hold a teaching job, well, there was no hope for a big eater like me. If that's what they wanted, so be it, but they should have hired somebody who didn't like noodles and dumplings in the first place. Here they were appointing me to the position without bothering to mention a word about it, and then they tell me that I'm not allowed to eat noodles and I'm not allowed to eat dumplings; this was a major blow to a fellow like me, who didn't have any other amusements. Then Redshirt piped up again: 'Middle school instructors belong, inherently, to the upper stratum of society. This being the case, the entertainments that they pursue should not be of an exclusively material nature. To devote themselves entirely to such pursuits cannot help but exert a negative influence on their characters. Being human, however, they can scarcely be expected to endure the rigors of provincial life without engaging in diversions of some sort. It is appropriate, therefore, for them to engage in amusements of an uplifting and spiritual nature, such as fishing, reading works of literature, composing haiku or poems in the modern style, and the like . . .'

As we sat there in silence, Redshirt went on spouting this nonsense, carried away by the sound of his own voice. If going out to fish for fertilizer, making silly jokes about goruki and Russian writers, watching your favorite geisha stand under a pine tree, or making up haiku about frogs jumping into old ponds qualified as spiritual amusements, well, so did eating tempura and wolfing down dumplings. He should have gone and tried washing that red shirt of his instead of preaching to us about those stupid diversions of his. By now I was so angry that I asked him, 'Is going to see the Madonna a spiritual amusement, too?' This time nobody laughed. They just looked around at each other with a strange expression as their eyes met. As for Redshirt, he stood there with his head hanging down and a pained look on his face. Take that! Got you that

time, didn't I? The only one I felt a little sorry for was the Pale
Squash, who had turned even paler than ever when he heard
these words.

7

I moved out of my lodgings that very night. As I was packing my things the landlady came in and inquired if anything was wrong. She also told me that if I was upset about anything, all I had to do was say so and they would make the necessary changes. That was a surprise! How did there get to be so many of these mixed-up people running around in the world? How was I supposed to know if she wanted me to leave or wanted me to stay? She was downright crazy. Getting into an argument with somebody like this would be a disgrace for any self-respecting Tokyo native, so I went out to find a man with a cart and left the place right away.

Leaving was easy enough, but I had no idea where to go. When the man asked where he should take my things, I told him to just keep quiet and follow me and he'd find out soon enough, and then set off at a lively pace. I thought the easiest thing would be to go back to Yamashiro-ya, but since I'd only have to leave again anyway, it would actually end up being more of a bother. If I just kept walking around I was bound to come across a boardinghouse or a place with a Room for Rent sign sooner or later. That, I figured, would be the place that fate had ordained for me. As I made my way through streets that looked like they'd be nice, quiet places to live, I ended up in Kajiyachō. This was where families of the samurai class had their mansions, not the part of town to find something like a boardinghouse in. Just as I was thinking I ought to head back toward a busier district, I suddenly had a good idea: my esteemed colleague the Pale Squash lived in this neighborhood. His family had occupied one of these mansions for generations, so he would be sure to know the area well. If I dropped in at his place and asked him about it, he might be able to come up with a promising suggestion. Luckily I'd already paid a call on him once before, so I had a pretty clear idea of how to get to his house, and I didn't have to spend a lot of time wandering around trying to find it. When I came to the house that I thought was probably the right one, I went up to the entrance and called out 'Excuse me!' twice. An elderly lady who looked to be about fifty appeared from inside holding an old-fashioned paper-wick lamp. Young women are fine with me, too, but somehow seeing an older one always gives me a good feeling. I guess it's because I like Kiyo so much, and it just seems to me that the same feeling must apply to old ladies everywhere. She was a dignified-looking lady with an old-fashioned widow's short haircut tied neatly in the back; since her features closely resembled the Squash's I assumed she was his mother. She invited me in politely, but I explained that I was just there to ask him a quick question about something and had her call him down to the doorway. When I told him about my situation and asked if he could think of any possibilities, he replied that this was indeed a predicament and stood there looking lost in thought for a while. Then he recalled that there was an elderly couple named Hagino who had a house on a street behind his, and they'd once told him that they had an empty parlor room and if he could recommend a reliable boarder they would be willing to rent it out since there was no point in letting it just sit there unoccupied. He wasn't sure if it was still available, he said, but we could go and have a look, and he kindly took me there.

From that night I boarded at the Haginos'. It came as a surprise, though, to find out that as soon as I moved out of Ikagin's the Hanger-on moved into my old room as if nothing could have been more natural. Even I was shocked by this news. I was beginning to wonder if the world consisted of nothing but scoundrels, each of them busily trying to put something over on everybody else. I was fed up.

It was depressing to realize that if this was the way people really were, I'd have to go along with it myself and not allow myself to be outdone by anybody. When you come right down to it, if living off the proceeds of pickpockets is the only way to get your three meals a day, you really have to wonder if it's really worth going on. On the other hand, if you go and hang yourself when you've got a good, healthy body it would be a disgrace to your ancestors, not to mention being bad for your reputation. Now that I thought about it, I would have been better off if I'd taken those six hundred yen and used them to set myself up as a milkman or some occupation like that instead of going to the Institute of Physical Sciences and learning something as useless as mathematics. If I had done that, Kiyo could have stayed with me, and I wouldn't have been stuck out here worrying about her. I hadn't noticed it when we were living together, but now that I had come to the country I finally realized what a good person she was. You could look all over Japan but you wouldn't find many women as good-natured as Kiyo. She had been suffering from a slight cold when I left Tokyo; now I wondered how she was getting on. She must have been really glad to get that letter I sent her. Still, I should have received a letter back from her by now . . . For two or three days thoughts like these filled my mind.

Since I was so concerned, I would sometimes ask the landlady if there were any letters for me from Tokyo, but she always gave me a pitying look and told me that nothing had come. The Haginos came from samurai stock, and as you might expect they were both people of quality, unlike my previous landlord and landlady. In the evenings the old man would practice chanting verses from the Noh plays in an odd voice, which was a little hard to take, but he never barged in and asked me if I'd like to have some tea, so things were a lot easier here. The old lady would sometimes come to my room and chat about this and that. Why, she wanted to know, hadn't I brought my wife with me and set up a household here? When I asked her if I really looked like a married man and informed her that I was, alas, still only twenty-three, she announced in her thick local dialect that 'It's perfectly natural that a man of twenty-three should have a wife, na moshi,' and then tried to make her point by bombarding me with half a dozen examples of men she knew who had gotten married at nineteen or had two kids by the age of twenty-one and the like. This was too much for me, so I

replied, in my best attempt at an imitation of her dialect, that if
it was really all right for a man of twenty-three to marry, I
wondered if she might help me find a suitable wife.

'Do you really mean it, na moshi?' she asked back.

'Yes, really really. I want to get married so badly I can't
stand it.'

'Yes, you would, wouldn't you, na moshi. That's the way
everybody feels when they're young.' I was at a loss for a reply
to this comment. 'But I'm positive that you already *have* a wife,
sir. You know, I've got it all figured out, na moshi.'

'Is that so? Very perceptive of you. And just how did you get
it all figured out?'

'How? Aren't you always aching to get a letter from Tokyo,
and asking me every day if anything has come yet, na moshi?'

'My, my. Most perceptive!'

'So I was right, wasn't I, na moshi?'

'Hmm, yes, maybe so.'

'But the young ladies today aren't like they used to be, you
know. You have to keep an eye on them these days, so you'd
best be on your guard, na moshi.'

'How's that? Are you telling me my wife has a lover in Tokyo?'

'Oh, no, *your* wife is fine, but . . .'

'Thank goodness, what a relief! But why should I be on my
guard, then?'

'Well, yours is fine . . . certainly yours is fine, but . . .'

'So where are the ones who aren't so fine?'

'There are plenty of them around here. You know that young
Tōyama lady, don't you, sir?'

'No, I don't.'

'You don't know who she is yet, na moshi? Now, she's the
best-looking young lady in these parts, na moshi. So good-looking,
in fact, that all the teachers at the school are always calling her
"the Madonna," na moshi. You haven't heard, na moshi?'

'So that's who the Madonna is? I thought they were talking
about some geisha.'

'No, no, it's one of those foreigners' words, it seems to be
their word for a lady who's good-looking, na moshi.'

'Ahh, that could be. My goodness!'

'I hear that she got that name from the art teacher, na moshi.'

'You mean the Hang— '

'Oh, no, it was Mr Yoshikawa that gave her that name, na moshi.'

'And this Madonna is one of the questionable ones?'

'This Madonna is a questionable Madonna, yes, na moshi.'

'What a shame. I see what you mean, though – any woman with a nickname has always been trouble.'

'Yes, that's true, na moshi. There was that Omatsu the Demon in the Kabuki play, and Ohyaku the Vampire, na moshi . . .'

'And the Madonna is like them?'

'That Madonna, na moshi, let me tell you – you know that Mr Koga from the school, the one that kindly brought you here, na moshi, well, she was all set to get married to him, but then, na moshi . . .'

'What? That's incredible. I never would have guessed the Squash was so blessed in his love life. It just goes to show, appearances can be deceiving – I suppose I'll have to be a little more careful.'

'But then last year Mr Koga's father passed away. Up till then they had plenty of money, plus they were shareholders in the bank, so everything was just fine, but once he was gone, I don't know what happened but all of a sudden things stopped going their way. The thing is, Mr Koga is just too nice a man for his own good, and so he was deceived, na moshi. The wedding kept being put off because of one thing or another, and then that Assistant Principal came along and asked for her hand, na moshi . . .'

'Redshirt, you mean? That scoundrel! I knew that shirt wasn't any ordinary fabric . . . Then what?'

'He had somebody go talk to the Tōyama family on his behalf. They said something to the effect that they wouldn't be able to respond right away seeing as they had a commitment with Mr Koga, but they would consider the proposal carefully, na moshi. Then Mr Redshirt found some people who were able to get him direct access to the Tōyama family. He began to be a frequent caller, and by and by he managed to win the young lady over, na moshi. Mr Redshirt did what he did, but the young lady also did what she did, and now nobody has a good word to say about her. There she was, already engaged to marry Mr Koga, and then when the college man comes along she switches over to him – it was an offense against the god who was watching over that day, I tell you!'

'Absolutely. Not just the god of that day, either – the god of the next day, and the one after that, it's an offense against all of them, for all time!'

'And then Mr Koga's friend Mr Hotta felt sorry for him, so he went to have a talk with the Assistant Principal. According to what I've heard, Mr Redshirt told him that he had no intention of snatching away a woman who was already engaged to somebody else. If that engagement were ever broken off he might seek the lady for himself, but for the present he was simply spending time with the Tōyama family and he didn't see how Mr Koga could possibly have any objection to that. Since there was nothing more that Mr Hotta could say at that point, he just went home. They say that the two of them have been on bad terms ever since, na moshi.'

'You certainly seem to know a lot about what's going on. I'm impressed! How do you manage to find out so much?'

'In a place this small, you hear about everything, na moshi.'

She heard about too much, from my point of view. At this rate she might know all about my tempura and dumpling incidents, too. This was no easy place to live in, but it did have its advantages: now I knew who the Madonna was, and I understood the relationship between the Porcupine and Redshirt, which would certainly come in handy later on. The only thing was, I still couldn't tell who the real bad guy was. Unless things are set out for me in clear black and white, it's hard for a simple type like me to figure out which side to take.

'Hmm . . . I wonder which one is the better person, Redshirt or the Porcupine . . .'

'Porcupine? What are you talking about?'

'That's what I call Mr Hotta.'

'Well, when it comes to strength Mr Hotta seems to be the stronger of the two, but Mr Redshirt is the one with the college degree, so he has the ability, na moshi. And when it comes to

who's nicer, Mr Redshirt is the nicer one, too, but I hear that
Mr Hotta is more popular with the students, na moshi.'

'So which one is better, then?'

'Well, the one with the higher salary must be the better one,
na moshi.'

I couldn't see any point in continuing with this conversation,
so I left things at that. A couple of days later I came back from
school to find the landlady waiting for me with a big smile. 'Ah,
you're finally home,' she said, and handed me a letter. As she
walked off, I saw that it was from Kiyo. There were a couple of
notes pasted on the envelope, from which I realized that it had
been forwarded from Yamashiro-ya to Ikagin's, and then from
Ikagin's to the Haginos'. I also realized that it had been kept at
Yamashiro-ya for about a week; I guess that being an inn they
put up letters there as well as people. When I opened it, I saw
that it was a really long one. Here's how it started:

Dear Botchan,
As soon as I got your letter I wanted to write back to you right
away, but unfortunately I was in bed for a week with a cold, so
it has taken me all this time to write. I'm sorry. Besides, I'm not
as good at reading and writing as the young ladies are these
days, so it's quite a strain for me to write even a clumsy letter
like this one. I was going to ask my nephew to write it for me,
but then I decided that since I was the one sending it, it wouldn't
be right if I didn't write it out myself, so I put everything I
wanted to say down on paper and now I'm making a clean copy.
It has only taken me two days to do this, but it took me four
days to get everything down the first time. I know that my writing may be hard for you to read, but this is the best I could do
so please read it through to the end.

The letter was on a single sheet of paper that was about four
feet long when you unfolded it all the way. She had written
about all kinds of things, and yes, it really was hard to read. It
wasn't just that her handwriting was bad: she had also run her
words and phrases so close together that it was a real strain to
figure out where one ended and another began. I'm such an

impatient type that normally there's no way I would be willing
to read through a letter that was so long and difficult, even if
somebody offered me five yen to do it. This one time, though, I
really concentrated and read it all the way through from beginning to end. But since I had to strain so hard just to make out
the individual words and phrases I couldn't work out what they
were supposed to mean when you put them together, so then I
had to start all over again from the beginning. By this time it
was getting dark inside the room, which made it even harder to
read than it was before, so I took it out to the veranda, sat
myself down on the edge, and read it through as carefully as I
could. The early autumn breeze was making the broad leaves of
the plantain quiver in the garden, and each time I felt it brush-
ing my skin it would also catch as much of the letter as I'd
unfolded and lift it gently in the air, so that by the time I'd read
it to the end the full four feet of it were rustling softly; it seemed
as if all I had to do was let it slip from my hands and it would
go drifting off toward the hedge on the far side of the yard. But
I was hardly in the mood to pay attention to such things,
because I was too absorbed in what Kiyo had to say, which
went as follows:

> Botchan, your character is as straight and clear as a length of
> split bamboo, but there's one thing I worry about, which is that
> you have too much of a temper . . . If you make up all kinds of
> nicknames for people it will give them a reason to resent you, so
> you've got to be careful about when and where you use them.
> You should only share them with me in your letters . . . I've
> heard bad things about country people, so make sure that you
> don't get yourself into any trouble . . . Even the weather must be
> less settled than it is in Tokyo, so take care not to get a chill and
> catch cold in your sleep. Because your letter was so short I
> couldn't get much of a picture of what things are like there, so
> next time please write me one that's at least half as long as this
> one . . . A five-yen tip for the people at the inn is fine if you don't
> run short later, just remember that when you're in the country
> the only thing you can count on is your money, so you have to
> spend as little as possible so that you'll have enough just in case

a time comes when you really need it . . . It must be hard if you haven't got any spending money, so I'm sending a money order for ten yen. I put the fifty yen you gave me in a postal savings account to help you out when you come back to Tokyo and get a house, but after I take out the ten yen there will still be forty so it should be all right . . .

Women, I couldn't help thinking, watch out for every little thing.

While I was sitting lost in my thoughts on the veranda with the letter fluttering in the breeze, Mrs Hagino opened the sliding door and brought me my dinner tray. 'Oh my,' she said, 'you're still reading your letter, na moshi? It certainly is a long one, isn't it, na moshi!' 'Yes,' I told her, 'it's an important one, so first I let it blow in the breeze for a while and then I read part of it, then I let it blow again and read some more.' Even I didn't know what this was supposed to mean. As usual, she had made boiled sweet potatoes for dinner. The Haginos were certainly treating me better than the people at Ikagin's had, and they were nicer people, with better manners, but unfortunately the food here was awful. Sweet potatoes again tonight – the same as last night, and the night before. It's true that I had announced that they were one of my favorite dishes, but I could hardly keep going on a diet of sweet potatoes and sweet potatoes alone. Here I had been laughing at my colleague the Pale Squash, but now it looked like I'd be turning into a Pale Potato myself any day. If Kiyo had been there she would have made me some nice tuna sashimi or the roasted fishcakes that I like, but in a poor, penny-pinching samurai household like this one there wasn't a chance. No matter how I looked at it, I needed to have Kiyo with me. If it seemed likely that I'd be staying on at that school for any length of time, I'd have her come down from Tokyo. Not allowed to eat a bowl of noodles and tempura? Not allowed to eat dumplings? Having to live as a boarder and be fed sweet potatoes till I started to turn yellow myself? Being a schoolteacher was a tough job – even Zen monks must eat like gourmets compared to this! After I polished off my plate I took two raw eggs out of my desk drawer, cracked the shells against the rim of my ricebowl, and slurped

them down, which finally gave me enough nutrition to keep me
going. How was I supposed to have the stamina to teach twenty-
one classes a week if I didn't fortify myself with raw eggs like
that?

Because of Kiyo's letter I was late going to the hot spring for
my bath. But by then I had become so accustomed to going every
evening that it wouldn't feel right if I missed even a single day.
I decided to take the train and headed out with my usual red
towel in hand, but by the time I got to the station I had missed
the train by a couple of minutes, so I took a seat on a bench to
wait for the next one. As I sat there smoking a cigarette, who
should turn up but the Squash. After what I had heard from Mrs
Hagino, I was feeling sorrier than ever for him. It had always
been kind of pitiful to see the way he kept such a low profile, as
if he was just some sort of trespasser in the universe, but pitiful
wasn't the word for it that night. I had just been thinking how
if it was in my power there was nothing I'd rather do than double
his salary, get him married to the Tōyamas' daughter, and send
them off to Tokyo for a month's holiday, so of course I gave him
a hearty greeting, asked him if he was also going to the hot
spring, and tried to give him my seat on the bench. The Squash,
whether out of politeness or whatever, just murmured 'Oh no,
please don't worry about me in the least' with an apologetic
look on his face, and went on standing there. I tried again, telling him that we'd be waiting for a while yet and he'd get tired
standing so he might as well sit down. The truth is, I was feeling
so sorry for him that I desperately wanted to get him to sit there
with me somehow or other. Finally he relented with a polite
'Well, then, begging your pardon.' What a world! There are
presumptuous types like the Hanger, who insist on sticking their
noses into places where it has no business being. There are guys
like the Porcupine who strut around with a look plastered on
their face announcing that Japan would be in trouble if they
weren't there. And then there are the ones like Redshirt who
convince themselves that they've got the markets in hair oil and
manly charm all cornered, or the Badger, whose attitude all but
proclaims that he is precisely what Education would look like
if it were ever to come to life and put on a frock coat. Every one

of them is puffed up in his own personal way, but I had never seen anyone like Mr Pale Squash, who tried so hard to be meek and unobtrusive that he looked more like a hostage puppet than a man. Sometimes he made you wonder if he really existed at all. It's true that his face was puffy, but if the Madonna had really thrown over an excellent man like him for Redshirt she had to be one hopeless hussy. Even if you put together a couple of dozen Redshirts, you couldn't hope to make such a fine husband out of them!

'Is anything wrong? You look rather worn out . . .'

'Oh, no, I'm not suffering from any particular complaints, but . . .'

'I'm glad to hear it. People aren't good for much when they're sick, are they?'

'*You* certainly seem to be a very healthy fellow.'

'Oh yes, I may be thin but I don't get sick. The thing is, I just can't stand being sick.'

The Squash grinned when he heard this.

Just then a burst of youthful-sounding feminine laughter rang out by the entrance to the platform. I turned around for a quick look, and what I saw was really something: a gorgeous woman, tall and fair-skinned, with a stylish hairdo, standing at the ticket counter with a matronly-looking lady in her mid-forties. I'm not any good at describing what makes a woman gorgeous, so I won't try, but this one was definitely absolutely gorgeous. Somehow just looking at her made me feel like I was cradling a ball of crystal that had been warmed in perfume in my palm. The older lady was shorter, but the resemblance in their faces was obvious: they had to be mother and daughter.

From the instant I got that first stunning glimpse I couldn't take my eyes off her. I had forgotten all about the Squash. But then, to my surprise, he suddenly got up and started walking over in the ladies' direction. This, I realized, might be the Madonna. The three of them exchanged casual greetings by the ticket counter, but they were too far away for me to make out any of the conversation.

I looked at the station clock and saw that we still had another five minutes to wait. Since I no longer had anyone to talk to, I was hoping that the train would come as soon as possible. Just then another passenger came hurrying into the station. It was Redshirt. He was wearing some kind of thin silk kimono with a carelessly wound crepe sash, with his gold watch chain dangling from it as usual. This item was a fake. Redshirt thought that nobody could tell and was always showing it off, but he couldn't fool me. As he dashed in, he looked nervously around the station, but when he saw the threesome talking in front of the ticket counter he gave them a polite bow and seemed to be exchanging a couple of words with them, but then he suddenly turned and floated over to where I was sitting with that little-cat-feet walk of his. 'Ah,' he said, 'so you're off to the springs, too? I was afraid I might miss the train so I rushed over, but I see that we still have a few minutes. I wonder if that clock is right . . .' As he pulled out his gold pocket watch and announced that there was two minutes' difference between it and the station clock, he took a seat beside me. Without so much as a glance back toward the ladies, he rested his chin on top of his walking stick and kept his gaze fixed straight ahead. The older lady looked over at him from time to time, but the young one never faced his way. Now I was sure she was the Madonna.

Finally a whistle shrieked and the train pulled in. The crowd on the platform jostled its way into the cars. Redshirt made a dash for the first-class seats. It wasn't as if going first class was anything to feel superior about: the first-class fare to the hot spring was five sen and second class was three, so there was only a difference of two sen between them. If even a person like me was willing to lay out the extra two sen for that white first-class ticket, which I was, you can see that there wasn't anything special about it. These country people seemed to be cheapskates, though; most of them rode second class, so paying two sen more or less must have been a big deal to them. The Madonna and her mother followed Redshirt into the first-class seats. The Squash would never even think of going first class. For a moment he stood at the doorway to the second-class seats with a hesitant look, but as soon as he noticed me he plunged right in. Feeling unbearably sorry for him, I followed him in. I figured that nobody would mind if somebody rode in second class with a first-class ticket.

At the hot spring, I ran into the Squash again after I came down into the bathing area in my robe. Even though I can barely squeeze a word out of my throat when it's my turn to speak at meetings and things, I'm usually pretty talkative by nature, and while we were sitting in the tub I kept trying to strike up a conversation with him. I just couldn't bear to see him looking so miserable. As a self-respecting Tokyo native, I thought, it was my duty to offer something, even if only a word or two, that might console the man in his hour of misery. Unfortunately, though, he just wouldn't join in. No matter what I said, all I could get out of him was an 'Ah' or an 'Umm,' and even coming up with those Ahs and Umms seemed to be a real strain, so eventually I gave up and excused myself.

I hadn't seen Redshirt in the bath. Of course there were any number of places to bathe at this spa, so even if we came on the same train, there was no reason to expect that we'd end up sharing the same tub. Coming out of the bathhouse, I noticed that the moon was looking particularly fine that night. There were willow trees planted on either side of the streets here, and their branches cast round shadows on the ground. I decided to take a little stroll. Up at the northern edge of town there was a big gate on the left; beyond it was a roadway that led to a Buddhist temple, but along the way on either side were the houses of a red-light district. Putting such establishments inside the precincts of a temple was surely a phenomenon without precedent. I wanted to go in and have a quick look around, but for all I knew it might end up getting me nailed by the Badger again at the next faculty meeting, so I decided not to and walked on by. Next to the gate was a small building with lattice windows and a dark curtain hanging in the doorway – it was the dumpling shop where I got myself into trouble before. There was a round lantern with the words SWEET BEAN SOUP and RICE CAKE SOUP hanging by the entrance, casting a patch of light on the trunk of a willow tree that was growing close to the eaves of the building. I would have loved to go in, but I resisted the temptation and walked on by.

Not being able to eat some dumplings when you wanted to felt pathetic. But to have your fiancée switch her affections to

another man was truly pathetic. Never mind the dumplings, I
realized – compared to the Squash, I wouldn't have had any
grounds for complaint even if I had to go without any food at
all for three days. Really, there's nothing in the world as unde-
pendable as human beings. Just looking at her face, you would
never have thought that such a gorgeous woman would be capable of doing anything so cruel, but she was; while Mr Koga
– puffy, pale, last-squash-on the-vine face and all – was a perfect
gentleman. You can never let your guard down. You think that
the Porcupine is a simple, honest fellow, and then you hear that
he's been stirring up the students . . . Then when you think he
was the one who was stirring them up, he urges the Principal to
give them the punishment they deserve . . . You think that
Redshirt is a walking mass of obnoxiousness, and then all of a
sudden he goes out of his way to be nice to you and warn you
about the danger you're in . . . and you find out that he's been
playing that game of his with the Madonna. And then he claims
that he has no designs on the woman unless her engagement to
Mr Koga falls through. Ikagin makes up excuses to get rid of
me, and then takes in the Hanger right away . . . However you
look at things, you just don't know what to believe. If I wrote
to Kiyo about all this I'm sure she'd be flabbergasted. Maybe
she'd say that it just goes to show that anyplace further away
than Hakone must be swarming with monsters.

I've always been pretty easygoing by nature, and up until now
I had always gotten by without letting anything bother me too
much, but in the mere month or so since I arrived in this town
I had suddenly come to see the world as a much scarier place.
Even though nothing particularly awful had happened to me, I
felt as if I had already aged a good five or six years. The best
thing to do would probably be to cut my stay here short and go
back to Tokyo . . . As these thoughts were running through my
mind, I found myself crossing a stone bridge and ending up on
the embankment along the Nozeri River. To call it a river may
make it sound sort of grand, but actually it was more like a
burbling brook, only about six feet across. About three-quarters
of a mile further down along the bank is a village called Aioi,
with a temple devoted to Kannon, the goddess of mercy.

I turned to look back toward town and saw its red lanterns shining in the moonlight. I could also hear the booming of giant *taiko* drums, which must have been coming from the red-light district. The current in the stream was shallow but swift, making it dance with a nervous-looking shimmer. I kept wandering aimlessly along the bank, and when I had come what I thought must have been about a quarter of a mile I could see some shadowy figures looming up ahead. The moonlight was bright enough for me to see that there were two of them. I thought they might be some young people from the village, on their way home after a visit to the hot spring. If so, you'd expect them to be singing some song as they went along, but they were surprisingly quiet.

I must have been walking faster than they were, and as I got closer the two shadows were gradually getting larger. One seemed to be a woman. As I came within about twenty yards of them, the man suddenly turned around. The moon was shining from behind me, so I could see his features pretty well. Ah-hah! The couple started walking again; I, with a certain plan in mind, followed after at full speed. Up ahead, the couple ambled along obliviously at the same leisurely pace they had kept up from the start. By now I could hear their voices so clearly I could almost reach out and touch them. The path along the riverbank was about six feet across, just barely wide enough for three people to walk abreast. I easily caught up with them, brushed past the man's sleeve, and then, after pulling two paces ahead of them, turned on my heel and looked the man straight in the face. The moonlight, without so much as a by-your-leave, clearly revealed my entire face, from my short-cropped hair to the tip of my chin. The man barely had time to get out a sharp 'Aa!' of recognition in a tiny voice and then turn toward his companion and mumble 'Let's head back' before the two of them were on their way back toward the hot spring area.

I wasn't sure if Redshirt had been trying to brazenly bluff his way out of it or if he had simply lost his nerve and run off without acknowledging me. One thing was for certain, though: I wasn't the only one who was getting himself into trouble in this little place.

8

Ever since that fishing trip with Redshirt, I had begun to have my suspicions about the Porcupine. When he had ordered me to get out of Ikagin's on some phony pretext, it only confirmed my belief that he was up to no good. But then at the meeting when he made that eloquent appeal to be strict with the students, he caught me off guard again and I didn't know what to think. And then when I heard from Mrs Hagino that he had tried to intervene on the Squash's behalf with Redshirt, I felt I really had to hand it to him. Just as I was starting to wonder if maybe the Porcupine wasn't the real bad guy after all, if maybe Redshirt was the rogue who had been planting a pack of plausible-sounding but unfounded suspicions and insinuations in my mind, there I was catching him taking the Madonna out for a walk along the Nozeri River. From that point on my mind was made up: Redshirt had to be the bad guy. Actually, I still wasn't quite sure if he was a bad guy or not, but you certainly couldn't call him a good one. Two-faced was what he was. If a man isn't as upright as a stalk of bamboo, you can't trust him. Even if you get into a fight with an upright man, you'll still have a good feeling about it. A guy like Redshirt – the mild-mannered, kindly, elegant type, always proudly showing off that amber pipe of his – that's the kind you'd better not trust, I believed, and also the kind you'd better not get into a fight with. And if by any chance you did get into a fight with him, it wouldn't be one you could feel good about, the way you could with a match in the sumo tournament back in Tokyo. Looking at it this way, the Porcupine – the guy with whom I'd gotten into that argument over a penny and a half that had the whole faculty room in an uproar – was more of a man by far. When he kept glaring at me with those deep-set eyes of his during the staff meeting I detested him, but afterward I realized that at least it was better than dealing with a smooth, slimy-voiced customer like Redshirt. In fact, after the meeting I had tried to make up with him once or twice, but the rascal wouldn't take me up on it; he just kept giving me that evil eye of his, so I got angry at him all over again and the standoff dragged on.

Ever since then the Porcupine wouldn't talk to me. The money I had put on his desk was still sitting there, gathering dust day by day. I wasn't about to touch it, of course, and he wasn't about to take it home with him either. On account of this one-and-a-half-sen barrier that stood between us, I couldn't say anything to him no matter how much I wanted to, and he kept his silence just as stubbornly. It had turned into a curse on the two of us. Eventually just coming into school and seeing those coins sitting there became a trial.

While the Porcupine and I still wouldn't have anything to do with each other, my relationship with Redshirt went on as before. The morning after the Nozeri River incident, as soon as I arrived at school he came over to my desk and started asking me all kinds of questions about how I liked my new lodgings and whether I wouldn't like to go on another fishing expedition for Russian literature and the like. I found this attitude of his a little obnoxious, so I mentioned something about how we had run into each other twice the night before. 'Yes,' he replied, 'at the station – umm, is that the time you always go out? On the late side, isn't it?' When I hit him with the news that I had also seen him by the Nozeri River, he said no, he hadn't been there, he'd gone straight home from the bathhouse. The liar! There shouldn't have been any need to hide it; I definitely had seen him there, after all. If a man like him was worthy of being the Assistant Principal of a middle school, well, I must be worthy of being the President of a university. From that time on I stopped trusting Redshirt. But while I was still on speaking terms with him, a man I didn't trust, I wasn't talking to the Porcupine, whom I now admired. This world is a very strange place.

One day Redshirt informed me that there was something he

wanted to discuss with me and asked me to visit him at home. This meant that I would have to take a day off from my regular routine of visiting the hot spring, which I regretted, but I set out around four o'clock anyway. Although Redshirt was still single, he had stopped living in a rented room long ago; now he occupied a house with an imposing entryway befitting his status as an Assistant Principal. The rent, I had heard, was nine and a half yen a month. As I stood there at the entrance, it occurred to me that if you could get a place like this for nine and a half yen in the country, I really ought to make Kiyo happy by splurging on one myself and bringing her down here from Tokyo. When I called inside, I was met at the door by Redshirt's younger brother. He was one of my students in arithmetic and algebra, and a very poor one. And as if that wasn't bad enough, since he was only an outsider here, his character left even more to be desired than those of the local yokels.

When I asked Redshirt what it was that he wanted to talk to me about, the great man pulled out that amber pipe of his and, as he puffed on some awful-smelling tobacco, made the following announcement: 'Since you started teaching for us, the students have been doing much better than they did under your predecessor, and the Principal is very pleased that we've acquired such a fine teacher. We're all counting on you, so I hope that you'll keep applying yourself to your work.'

'Is that so? Well, as far as applying myself goes, I don't see how I can do any more than I'm already doing . . .'

'The way you're doing things now is fine. I just hope that you won't forget about that little matter that we talked about a while back.'

'Do you mean that business about getting myself into some real trouble with someone who was helping me find a place to live?'

'Well, if you put it in such explicit terms it loses all meaning, but . . . well, be that as it may . . . I think you understand the basic point I'm getting at here, so . . . Anyway, if you continue to keep up the good work, the school always takes notice of such things, so before too long, as soon as we have the wherewithal, I think that we should be able to do something for you in the way of remuneration . . .'

'Oh? Are you talking about a raise? I'm really not concerned with that kind of thing, but of course if I *could* get one, then so much the better . . .'

'Well, it just so happens that one of our instructors will be transferring out soon – of course, I'll have to talk to the Principal about it so I can't guarantee anything yet, but we might be able to take advantage of some of the savings on his salary. Anyway I'm planning to ask the Principal to see what he can do for you.'

'Thank you very much. And who is it that's being transferred?'

'Well, since the announcement is going to be made shortly, I suppose it's all right to tell you now. Actually, it's Mr Koga.'

'What? Koga? But isn't this his hometown?'

'It's true that he is from here, but due to certain circumstances . . . it was partly at his own request.'

'Where is he going?'

'To Nobeoka, in Miyazaki Prefecture. Since it's such a remote place, he'll be getting a one-step raise in his pay.'

'Will somebody be coming to take his place?'

'We've pretty much decided on who his successor will be. Based on how things work out with him, we should be able to do something for you.'

'That's fine. There's no need to go out of your way to get me a raise, though.'

'Anyway I will be talking to the Principal. And I think that he sees this the same way that I do, but eventually we may also have to ask you to do something more for us. I do hope that you'll be ready and willing.'

'You mean I'll have to teach more classes?'

'No, in fact you might end up with fewer classes, but . . .'

'I'd be working more, but teaching less? That sounds sort of strange . . .'

'Yes, it may sound a little strange . . . it's rather hard to go into the specifics right now, but, well, basically, what I'm getting at is that we may be asking you to take on a greater responsibility.'

I didn't get it at all. A 'greater responsibility' would probably mean becoming the head mathematics teacher, but that was the Porcupine's job, and there was no need to worry about that character resigning any time soon. What's more, since he was the students' favorite, it certainly wouldn't be a good idea for the school to transfer him or fire him. It was always hard to see what Redshirt was really getting at when he told you something, but at least we had now covered the business that we needed to talk about. As we chatted on a little about this and that, he brought up the topic of the Squash's farewell party, and then the question of whether I was a drinker, and then something about what a lovable gentleman the Squash was. Finally, he changed the subject completely and hit me with a question about whether I ever composed haiku. This sounded like trouble, so I told him that I didn't, said goodbye, and headed home on the spot. Haiku is either for masters like Bashō, or for guys like hair stylists. What business does a math teacher have fooling around with little poems about morning glories and the bucket at the well?

When I got back home, I tried to figure it all out. There was just no accounting for some of the people you find in this world. Even if the Squash had, for some reason, had enough of this hometown of his where he was all set up with both a family house and a job at the school, I couldn't see why he would want to go off and make life harder for himself in an unfamiliar part of the country. If he was going to some fine metropolis, the kind of place where at least there were trains running, it wouldn't have been so bad. But Nobeoka? It hadn't even taken me a month to get my fill of *this* place, which at least could be reached easily enough by boat. Nobeoka, on the other hand, is all the way out in the middle of a bunch of mountains – which are in the middle of another bunch of mountains, which are in the middle of even more mountains. According to Redshirt, you get off a boat, then there's a day's journey by horse-drawn wagon to the city of Miyazaki, and then it's another full day's wagon ride from there. Just hearing the name of the place makes you think that it couldn't be very civilized. It sounds like a town where the inhabitants must be divided about evenly between monkeys and humans. What kind of whim would make anybody, even somebody as unworldly as the Squash, want to go out there and associate with a bunch of monkeys?

Back at the house, the landlady brought me my meal as usual.

'Sweet potatoes again today?' I asked. No, she said, today it was tofu, na moshi. Not that there was that much difference between the two.

'I hear that Mr Koga is moving to Nobeoka.'

'Yes, the poor man, na moshi!'

'Poor man? If he wants to go, there's nothing more to say, is there?'

'Wants to go? Who wants to, na moshi?'

'Who wants to, na moshi? *He* does! He must be doing this on some kind of whim, no?'

'You've been good and hoodwinked, I see. It's not like that at all, na moshi.'

'You don't say? Well, Redshirt just told me so. If I've been good and hoodwinked, then Redshirt must be a lying hoodlum.'

'Of course that's what he would tell you – but naturally Mr Koga doesn't really want to go either, na moshi.'

'In other words, you believe both of them. Very even-handed of you. But what in heaven's name is going on?'

'This morning Mr Koga's mother came over, and eventually she told me the whole story, na moshi.'

'And what is the whole story she told you?'

'Ever since her husband died, the Kogas haven't been as well off as people think, and now that things have become hard for them she went to see the Principal and asked him if he couldn't arrange to have her son's salary increased a bit, seeing as how he had been teaching at the school for four years now.'

'I see.'

'The Principal said that he'd give the idea careful consideration, so Mrs Koga left feeling that things would be all right now. Then she waited to hear that the raise had come through. She was hoping that it would take a month or so, but what actually happened was that one day the Principal called Mr Koga in and told him that unfortunately the school didn't have any money to give him a raise. However, he'd been notified that there was an opening in Nobeoka, with a salary five yen higher than what he was making here. This, he thought, sounded like just what Mr Koga had been looking for, so he'd gone ahead and filled out the papers and now Mr Koga should get ready to go.'

'That sounds more like an order than a proposal!'

'That's right. Mr Koga would rather have stayed where he was than go away somewhere for higher pay. He asked the Principal not to transfer him since he has a house here as well as his mother, but the Principal told him it was all decided already, and they had even hired a teacher to replace him, so he had to go.'

'But that's terrible! What a trick to play on somebody! So Koga really didn't want to go after all . . . I kept thinking it just didn't make any sense. Going out in the wild and living with the monkeys, just for another five yen a month? Who would be such a dunce?'

'Dunce? But he's a teacher, na moshi!'

'All right, call him whatever you want . . . But anyway, Redshirt has to be behind this scheme. What a rotten thing to do – a real sucker punch! No wonder he says there's no problem with giving *me* a raise. But if they think I'm going to accept it now, they've got another think coming!'

'Will you be receiving a raise, na moshi?'

'They say I will, but I think I'll turn it down.'

'Why would you do that, na moshi?'

'I just will, no matter what. Let me tell you, that Redshirt is a fool. And a rat.'

'Even if he is, if he offers you a raise you'd be better off taking it, no questions asked, na moshi. When you're young you get upset about all kinds of things, but then later on you realize that you were only getting yourself into more trouble that way and you should have controlled yourself. The only person you hurt by losing your temper is you, and you'll end up regretting it. That's the way it is, so take this old lady's advice – if Redshirt says he's going to give you a raise, just say thank you and accept it.'

'Listen, I don't need an old lady like you telling me what to do when it's none of your concern. It's my salary, no matter how much it goes up, or down, and mine alone.'

She left the room without another word. Her husband was chanting a passage from some Noh play in a relaxed, mellow voice. The whole point of Noh chanting seems to be to take some lines that you could understand perfectly well on paper and recite them in a ridiculously complicated way to make sure that nobody can understand them any more. How he managed to practice that stuff every night without getting thoroughly sick of it was a mystery to me. Anyhow I had much bigger things to worry about. They'd told me that they were going to give me a raise. It wasn't as if I'd especially wanted one, but I figured that it would have been a waste to let them leave the money sitting around doing nothing, so I'd accepted. But would I be mean enough to take a cut out of the salary of somebody who had been forced to accept a transfer when he really didn't want to go? What the hell did they think they were doing banishing the man to the wilds of Nobeoka when he had told them that all he wanted was to stay right here? Even when a famous exile like Sugawara no Michizane was sent to Kyushu, he was allowed to settle in a place no more remote than the outskirts of Fukuoka. And hadn't Kawai Matagoro, a notorious murderer, also ended up in a fairly civilized part of the island like Sagara? Anyway, I'd never forgive myself if I didn't go to Redshirt and refuse the raise.

I changed into a formal outfit and went out. When I stood in that spacious entryway of his and announced my presence, the same brother came out to greet me, this time with a look that said 'What? You again?' Well, I was ready to come as many times as I needed to; if I had to get them out of bed in the middle of the night, so be it. Did he really think I was just there to pay some kind of idle social call? I was there to give my salary back, whether they liked it or not. The brother told me that Redshirt was with another visitor at the moment; I answered that I would just like to talk with him briefly, even if it was only there in the doorway. He went back inside. Looking down at the floor, I noticed a pair of slender wooden sandals with an inlay of woven rush on the tops. From inside the house I could hear a voice saying 'Well, then, it's time to celebrate – banzai!' The visitor, I realized, had to be the Hanger-on – that high-pitched voice and the artsy footwear couldn't have belonged to anybody else.

Eventually Redshirt appeared with an oil lamp in his hand and invited me in, announcing that the other caller was none other than Mr Yoshikawa. I declined and told him that all I wanted was a quick word with him, which I could have right there. His face was as red as a beet. He must have been having a drink with the good old Hanger.

'About what you said before about giving me a raise: I'm here to tell you that I've been thinking it over, and I've decided not to accept it.'

Redshirt pushed the lamp out in front of him and studied my face from within the shadows. Caught off guard and at a loss for a reply, he stood there in a daze. Maybe he couldn't believe that he had just encountered the one and only guy in the whole world who would actually turn down a raise, or maybe he just couldn't imagine why, even if somebody was going to turn it down, they had to come back to announce it so soon after they had walked out the door, or maybe it was some combination of the two, but anyway he just stood there, his mouth looking kind of peculiar as he struggled to get it to work.

'When I accepted that raise before, it was because I thought that Mr Koga was transferring voluntarily, but . . .'

'Koga certainly did request a kind of transfer.'

'That's not what happened. He wants to stay here. Even if he doesn't get a raise, he wants to stay in his hometown.'

'Is that what he told you?'

'Well, I didn't hear it directly from him.'

'Well whom did you hear it from, then?'

'From my landlady – who heard it from his mother. She told me about it today.'

'So that's the story the old lady at your place told you, then?'

'Well, yes.'

'Pardon me for saying so, but something is a bit out of order here. According to what you're telling me, I get the impression that you believe what your old landlady tells you, but you don't believe what your Assistant Principal tells you. Is that the way I'm supposed to understand it?'

He had me there. You really have to hand it to these college men. They know just how to latch on to some point that you'd never thought of and then keep rubbing it in. My old man always used to tell me that I was hopelessly impulsive. Now I could see what he meant. When I heard what my landlady had to say I was so shocked that I sprang right into action, but I hadn't made any effort to get a full account from the Squash or his mother. So now here I was in a bind, finding it not so easy to parry this collegiate-style attack.

It wasn't easy to parry directly, but in my own heart I had already issued a declaration of no confidence in Redshirt. My old landlady may have been a grasping cheapskate, but at least she wasn't a liar or a hypocrite like him. All I could say was this: 'What you say may well be true, but all the same I do not wish to receive a raise.'

'This is getting stranger and stranger. First you tell me that you've come expressly to inform me that due to certain circumstances that you've heard about you can't accept a raise; then, even though I've explained that there's no basis to what you've heard, you insist on rejecting it anyway. I really don't know what to make of this.'

'Perhaps you don't, but anyway I refuse.'

'If it bothers you that much I won't go so far as to force it on you, but doing a complete about-face like this in the space of just two or three hours will have an effect on your credibility in the future.'

'That's all right with me.'

'Well, it shouldn't be. There's nothing more important in life than trust. Even if I were to concede, just for argument's sake, that the landlord at your— '

'The landlady, not the landlord.'

'Either way. Anyhow, even if we were to suppose that what the old lady told you was true, the money for your raise isn't being taken out of Koga's salary, is it? He goes off to Nobeoka. His replacement arrives, and goes to work for slightly less pay. We're simply assigning the differential to you, so there's really no need for you to feel sorry for anyone. Koga will be better off in Nobeoka, and the new man is committed to working for less from the beginning. So if this allows your pay to go up, I don't see how things could have worked out any better. If you still object, so be it, but why don't you go home and think it all over carefully one more time?'

I can't boast much about my brainpower, so normally if some-body subjects me to a smoothly polished line of talk like this, I'll give in and concede that it might very well be true and that I'm the one who'd been in the wrong – but not that night. Ever since I first got to town, there was something about Redshirt that had rubbed me the wrong way. At one point I had changed my mind and decided that he was a kindhearted fellow in a feminine sort of way, but now, when it was becoming clear that there was really nothing kind about him at all, that backlash effect just made me dislike him all the more. So no matter how powerfully he laid out those fine and logical arguments of his, no matter how hard he tried to overwhelm me with his Assistant Principalian grandeur, I didn't care. Just because somebody can out-argue you, that doesn't necessarily make them a good person. And the person who gets out-argued isn't necessarily a bad person, either. To all appearances, what Redshirt had to say made perfect sense, but splendid as it sounded, that still didn't give it the power to seduce you deep down in your heart. If you could really win people's hearts over with the power of money, author-ity, or reasoning, then moneylenders, policemen, and college professors would be more popular than anybody else. There was no way that my heart was going to be swayed by the logic of some middle school Assistant Principal. People operate on their likes and dislikes, not on logic.

'What you have to say is perfectly true, but I don't want that raise any more; anyway, I won't accept it. Thinking it over won't change a thing. Goodbye.' As I went back through the gate, I noticed the Milky Way streaming across the sky overhead.

9

When I went to school on the morning of the day of the fare-well banquet for the Pale Squash, the Porcupine suddenly offered me this long-winded apology:

'The other day when Ikagin came and told me that you were just too rough for them, and then asked me to do them a favor and see if I could get rid of you, I took him at his word. But later I found out that he's actually a shady character who goes around selling fake paintings stamped with phony seals, so I realized that what he said about you must have been false as well. When he saw that you weren't going to have anything to do with him and he wouldn't be able to make any money off you by selling you some scrolls and antiques, he came up with that cock-and-bull story of his. I didn't know what kind of man he was, and I hope you can forgive me for having treated you so badly.'

Without a word I picked up the one and a half sen which were still sitting on the Porcupine's desk and put them in my coin purse. 'You're taking them back?' he asked incredulously. 'Yeah,' I explained, 'I didn't want to accept any favors from you so I was determined to return your money, but when I thought things over later I decided that it was better to accept after all, so I'm taking these back.' The Porcupine broke into a loud guffaw and asked 'Well, in that case why didn't you do it sooner?' When I told him that actually I'd been meaning to do it for a long time, but somehow it felt funny so I just left the coins sitting there, and that lately I'd been feeling so bad about it that I dreaded the idea of coming to school, he said that I was obvi-ously the kind of guy that just couldn't stand giving in to

anybody. You're a pretty stubborn case yourself, I shot back.
Then came the following exchange:

'So where are you from, anyway?'

'I'm an Edokko – Tokyo born and Tokyo bred.'

'Ah, an Edokko. No wonder you hate to give in.'

'And what about you?'

'I'm from Aizu.'

'Aizu, huh? That explains it. Stubborn! Are you going to the
farewell banquet?'

'Sure. What about you?'

'Of course I am. I'm even planning to go down to the harbor
to see him off when he leaves.'

'It's going to be an interesting party. Just you wait and see.
I'm ready to drink up a storm.'

'Suit yourself. I'm going to have myself something to eat and
then get right out of there. People who drink are idiots.'

'You don't waste any time when it comes to picking fights,
do you. Typical Edokko hothead!'

'Whatever. Anyhow, can you stop by my place on your way
over tonight? There's something I want to talk to you about.'

He came by as requested. What I wanted to tell him was this:
every time I caught sight of the Squash lately I felt so sorry for
him that I could barely stand it, but now that the time to say
goodbye had finally come I felt even more miserable – so much
so that I would have been glad to go in his place if I could. I was
thinking I'd like to make a big speech at the banquet and give
him a really splendid send-off, but with my rough-cut Tokyo
style of talking I'd never be able to make it sound right, so it
occurred to me that I'd be better off if I could get the Porcupine
to do the talking; with that booming voice of his he ought to be
able to scare Redshirt right out of his wits.

I started off by bringing him up to date on the Madonna situation, but of course he knew more about it than I did. I told him
about what I'd seen by the Nozeri River and how I thought that
Redshirt was a total idiot, to which he replied by accusing me of
calling everybody I met an idiot. Hadn't I called people like him
the very same thing just that morning in school? If he was an idiot,
he added, then Redshirt certainly couldn't be one, because they

had nothing in common. All right, I said, in that case Redshirt was a gutless nincompoop, to which the Porcupine immediately agreed. No matter how tough he was, the Porcupine was no match for me when it came to knowing a lot of juicy insults. I guess that Aizu people don't have a lot to offer in that department.

Then I brought up the issues of my pay raise and Redshirt's remarks about assigning me some heavier responsibilities. 'In that case, he must be planning to get rid of me,' the Porcupine said with a snort. When I asked him if he was willing to be relieved of his duties, he said absolutely not, and haughtily announced that if he was going to be relieved, he would make sure that Redshirt went with him. But when I came back at him with the question of just how he intended to get Redshirt relieved, he admitted that he hadn't considered that part yet. The man certainly looked strong, but as far as brainpower went it seemed he didn't have that much going for him. Then I explained how I had turned down that offer of a pay raise, which made him very happy: 'Just leave it to an Edokko to pull off something like that! Well done!'

I asked him how come he hadn't stepped in to try and keep the Squash here when it was so obvious that he didn't want to leave. By the time the Squash had told him about it, he said, everything had already been settled. He had tried appealing to the Principal twice and to Redshirt once, but nothing could be done. Anyway, he continued, part of the problem was that Koga was simply too nice a person. When Redshirt broke the news to him, he should have refused outright, or said that he would think it over at least, but instead he let himself be taken in by all that smooth talk and accepted it on the spot, so that when his mother went to plead his case later, and when the Porcupine himself went to make his appeal, it was totally useless. All very regrettable.

The whole thing, I suggested, was probably nothing more than a scheme by Redshirt to get the Squash out of the picture so that he could get his hands on the Madonna himself. No doubt about it, said the Porcupine: that guy may look harmless enough, but he's always got some cunning scheme up his sleeve, and when anybody calls him on it, he's got his escape route all figured out in advance. A truly shifty customer. The only way to deal with somebody like that is to beat it out of him, he continued, rolling up his sleeve and showing me the muscles on his brawny arm. 'Pretty powerful-looking,' I said. 'Do you practice jujitsu?' 'Just feel this,' he said, and flexed his bicep. I gave it a squeeze. It felt as hard as the pumice stone that you rub your skin with at the bathhouse.

I was so impressed that I told him that with arms like those he could probably beat up five or six Redshirts at a time. 'Beyond a doubt,' he said, bending and unbending his arm as the lump in his bicep rippled up and down beneath the skin. I really enjoyed watching this display. According to him, if you tied a thick cord of twisted paper tightly around his arm, he could snap it simply by flexing that bicep of his. When I said that I could probably do the same thing myself, he said 'You think so? Well, why don't you go ahead and try it, then?' Better not to take up the challenge, I decided, since it would have been pretty embarrassing if it turned out that I couldn't do it after all.

'How about it,' I asked, just for fun, 'are you ready to give Redshirt and the Hanger-on a nice working over after you've done your drinking tonight?' The Porcupine gave this idea some thought, but finally said no, tonight was not the night. When I asked why not, he pointed out that it wouldn't be fair to Koga, and besides, if he was going to give them a beating, it would have to be some time when he had caught them red-handed doing something bad, so that he wouldn't look like the offending party. This all sounded quite sensible. The Porcupine, slow-witted as he was, still seemed capable of being more thoughtful than I was.

'Well, then,' I said, 'when you make your speech, be sure to say all kinds of good things about the Squash. If *I* tried it, it would just sound like Edokko chatter, too lightweight to do him justice. And besides, whenever I'm on the spot and have to come out and say my piece, I suddenly feel like there's a big wad of something stuck in my throat and I get all choked up and can't get a word out – so I'm counting on you.' 'That's a strange kind of condition,' the Porcupine mused. 'So, you can't express yourself in company? That must be a problem.' No, I said, it really wasn't a problem at all.

By and by the time came for the Porcupine and me to set off for the banquet. It was being held at a restaurant called Kashin-tei, which was supposed to be the fanciest in town. I had never set foot in the place before. I had heard that the building used to be the mansion of one of the senior retainers of the local feudal lord; later it had been sold off and turned into a restaurant with a minimum of remodeling, and it certainly did retain an imposing appearance. Converting a senior retainer's residence into an eating-and-drinking establishment seemed a little like taking a warrior's magnificent battle robe and turning it into underwear as far as I was concerned.

By the time we arrived most of the others were already there, scattered in groups of two or three in a thirty-foot-square banquet room. As you might expect in such a grand room, the decorative alcove was wonderfully spacious, too; even the alcove in my old room at the inn simply didn't compare. This one measured a full twelve feet across. On the right side was a Seto ware vase with a red pattern, holding a large pine branch. I wasn't sure what the point of using a pine branch as a decoration was, but I suppose they were trying to be economical and chose something that would keep its leaves for a couple of months. I asked the science teacher where he thought that piece of Seto ware came from. 'That's not Seto, it's Imari,' he announced. When I told him that I thought that Imari was a kind of Seto ware, he just laughed. Later I found out that the term Seto ware strictly refers to pottery made in a place called Seto. Being an Edokko, I had just assumed it was the name for all kinds of ceramics. In the middle of the alcove was a big hanging scroll, with something written in four lines of seven Chinese characters, each of them as big as my face. It looked very poorly done to me. I couldn't understand why such an ugly piece was being displayed so prominently, but when I asked the Chinese classics teacher about it, he informed me that it was the work of a famous calligraphy master named Kaioku. Kaioku or whatever, I still think it was badly done.

Eventually the secretary, Kawamura, asked us to take our seats. Since we were sitting on the floor, I chose a spot that had a pillar behind it that I'd be able to lean my back against. The

Principal, attired in a formal kimono with ceremonial skirt and
jacket, occupied the seat of highest rank, directly in front of the
Kaioku scroll. Redshirt, in a similar outfit, occupied the place
to his left. To his right was the guest of honor, the Pale Squash,
also in Japanese dress. I was in a Western suit, which made it
uncomfortable for me to sit in the formal position with my legs
folded under me, so I promptly began sitting with my knees
crossed. Next to me was the physical education teacher, in black
trousers, sitting in a proper formal position; as you would expect
from somebody who taught that subject, his self-discipline
showed. Finally the trays with our meals were brought out. There
were flasks of saké, too. The teacher who was in charge of
making the arrangements rose and delivered some brief intro-
ductory remarks. Then the Badger rose, followed by Redshirt.
Each of the three offered his own parting tribute but, in such a
similar style it made you wonder if they hadn't coordinated the
whole thing in advance, they all proclaimed their admiration for
the Squash's stellar qualities as an educator and as a human
being, followed by expressions of profound regret at his impend-
ing departure and the great loss that it represented not only for
the school but on a personal level, and protestations that as it
had been his earnest desire to obtain a transfer due to various
personal circumstances, they were left with no alternative but
to honor his wishes. None of them showed the slightest sense
of shame at uttering such barefaced lies at a farewell banquet.
Redshirt was the most effusive of all – he even had the audacity
to claim that the loss of such a fine friend was a great personal
misfortune for him. Moreover, since his remarks sounded so
convincing, and were delivered in a tone that was dripping with
even more gentility than usual, anybody who happened to be
listening to him for the first time would undoubtedly have been
taken in. This must have been the way he got the Madonna to
fall for him, too. Midway through this farewell speech of
Redshirt's, the Porcupine flashed me a withering glance from
across the way. I silently signaled back my own disgust by pulling my lower eyelid down with my finger.

No sooner had Redshirt taken his seat than the Porcupine
shot up as if he'd hardly been able to wait for this moment to

come. Impulsively I began to clap my hands in glee, but as the entire assembly, from the Badger on down, turned their eyes in my direction, it made me feel a little uneasy. The Porcupine's speech, which I had been anticipating so eagerly, went like this:

'We have just heard, first from our Principal and especially from our Assistant Principal, how deeply they regret the transfer of Mr Koga. I, however, take a somewhat different view: I look forward eagerly to his departure from this place, and as quickly as possible. Nobeoka is indeed a remote location, and in comparison with our town it may present some inconveniences from a material point of view. But from what I have heard, its ways remain simple and unspoiled, and the faculty and student body there all retain the plain and solid virtues of olden days. In such a place you will find, I believe, not a single fashionable knave who showers you with false-hearted flattery, or seeks to use his pleasing features to mislead a gentleman. In such a place a warm-hearted, virtuous person like yourself will be certain to be welcomed with open arms by all. Therefore, Mr Koga, I heartily congratulate you on the occasion of this auspicious transfer. Finally, I would like to offer a humble wish that once you have established yourself in Nobeoka, you will as soon as possible find yourself a well-bred young lady, one who is qualified to serve as a suitable companion to a true gentleman, and proceed to establish a harmonious home and family with her, and by so doing bring mortal shame upon a certain fickle and faithless hussy. Ah-hemm, ah-hemm . . .'

Having cleared his throat noisily a couple of times, the Porcupine sat back down. I wanted to clap again but, afraid of attracting everybody's attention again, I held back. After the Porcupine the next to rise to speak was the Squash himself. Leaving his own seat and walking down to the spot reserved for the lowest-ranking member on the opposite side of the room, he politely offered his salutations to the audience and then proceeded to declare that 'In all sincerity I can find no words to adequately express how deeply moved I am by this magnificent send-off which my esteemed colleagues have been so kind as to bestow upon me on the occasion of my relocation, due to personal circumstances, to Kyushu. In particular, I am most grateful for the unforgettable farewell messages which I have just received from the Principal, the Assistant Principal, and others. As I prepare to embark on a journey to a distant place, it is my hope that you will not banish me from your thoughts, and will continue to favor me with the same generous support that you have so kindly conferred upon me in the past.' Then, with a profound and humble bow, he returned to his seat. It seemed that there was virtually no limit to the goodness of the man's character. Here he was deferentially expressing his gratitude to the Principal and Assistant Principal who had been playing him for a fool. This would have been remarkable enough even if it had only been a matter of empty formalities, but judging from the way he held himself, the words he used, and the expression on his face, you would have to say that his emotions were genuine. To be offered the sincere appreciation of a man as saintly as this should have been enough to inspire feelings of pity and shame in anybody, but the Badger and Redshirt just sat there and soaked it all up with a straight face.

Once the speeches were over, the next sounds to be heard were the slurping noises that arose all around the room as everyone began attacking their soup. I gave it a try too, but it tasted awful. There were also some pieces of fish cake, but they had a strange, smudgy color that made them look as though somebody had tried to roast them but given up halfway through. There was sashimi, too, but the slices had been cut so coarsely that they might just as well have served us slabs of raw tuna steak. My fellow guests on both sides, apparently undeterred, were busy devouring everything as if this was some kind of splendid feast. I guess they had never had a chance to try the kind of fresh fish we enjoy in Tokyo.

In due course flasks of heated saké started to be passed around one after another, and all over the room the mood promptly took on a livelier tone. The Hanger-on made straight for the Principal's seat and reverentially accepted a drink from him. What a creep! The Squash went from one guest to the next and exchanged drinks with each of them; apparently he was intending to make his way around the entire room. This was really above and beyond the call of duty. When he came to my place he politely straightened out the pleats of his formal kimono skirt and requested the honor of sharing a cup with me. Painfully I folded my trousered legs into a formal seated position and poured. 'What a shame,' I said, 'that we have to say goodbye so soon after I've arrived. When do you leave? I hope you won't mind if I go down to the harbor to see you off.' The Squash answered that I shouldn't bother, since I was undoubtedly very busy. Regardless of what he said, though, I was determined to take time off from school and go see him off.

By the time an hour or so had passed, things were starting to drift out of control. A couple of people were already pretty tipsy: 'Go on, have yourshelf another drink . . . No no, I told *you* to have one, I inshisht . . .' This was becoming a little tedious, so I excused myself and headed for the bathroom. As I stood in the courtyard admiring the old-fashioned garden by the light of the moon, the Porcupine appeared. 'How about it, pretty good speech, wasn't it?' He was obviously quite pleased with himself. I agreed that it was excellent, but there was one comment that I did object to. When he asked me what it was, I answered, 'Didn't you say something about not finding a single fashionable knave in Nobeoka, somebody who would use his pleasing features to mislead a gentleman?'

'So?'

'"Fashionable knave" didn't go far enough.'

'Well, what should I have said, then?'

'You should have told him that he wouldn't find a single fashionable knave – or swindler, or weasel, or sneak thief, or flimflam man, or snake-oil salesman, or stool pigeon, or any characters so low that you couldn't tell the difference between them and a dog if you heard them say "Woof!" . . .'

'I couldn't have come up with all that if I tried. You're the one who has a way with words. I mean, what a vocabulary! I can't believe that you're no good at making speeches.'

'Come on, that's all just stuff that I keep stored in my head so that I'll have it good and ready in case I ever get into a fight. You can't use words like that when you're making a speech.'

'Hmm, I wonder. Anyway, you really know how to pour it on. Let's hear that one more time.'

'As many times as you want: fashionable knave or swindler or weasel . . .' Just as I was getting warmed up, a pair of figures suddenly came staggering toward us, thumping their way along the boards of the courtyard veranda.

'Hey! Whadda you two think you're doing running out on ush like that? We're not gonna let you get away sho easily . . . C'mon, now, drink up! . . . Weasels, huh? Hey, I like that . . . C'mon . . . weasel all have a drink together . . .'

Before we knew it, they were busy pulling us back inside. Actually, the two of them must have come out to look for the bathroom, but I guess they were too drunk to remember about that when they started dragging us in. It seems that drunks can get so distracted by anything that happens to be in front of their nose at the moment that they forget all about whatever it was they were trying to do before.

'Look here, gen'lmen! Weasel just pulled these two back in! Now give them shomething to drink . . . Weasel get these weasels sho drunk they'll shay weeee . . . can't drink any more!! Now, don't you run out on us!'

They pinned me flat against the wall, even though I wasn't even trying to run out. I looked around the room and saw that there wasn't a single tray left with anything to eat on it. Some people, after they had finished off everything on their own tray, had set off on raiding parties and were cleaning out others a dozen yards away. Somewhere along the line, the Principal had disappeared.

At this point in the proceedings, a group of three or four geisha stuck their heads in the room and inquired, 'Is this the place?' This was a bit of a surprise, but since I was still pinned against the wall all I could do was stand there and observe the scene. Redshirt, who had been leaning against one of the pillars by the alcove with a self-satisfied look as he puffed on that amber pipe of his, sprang to his feet and made a sudden move for the door, but when he crossed paths with the geisha as they came into the room, one of them, the youngest and prettiest-looking, stopped and greeted him with a smile. They were too far away for me to hear what she was saying, but it seemed to be nothing more than 'Oh, my! Good evening!' Redshirt just ignored her and sailed on out of the room; that was the last we saw of him for the night. I guess he must have followed the Principal's lead and gone home.

With the arrival of the geisha the atmosphere immediately got very jolly indeed, and the noise level shot way up as well: it sounded like everybody was shouting at once to welcome the ladies into the fun. One guy tried to play some kind of guessing game with them, yelling at the top of his lungs, the way fencers in a quick-draw contest do when they're trying to intimidate the opposition. Closer to me some other guys were totally engrossed in a game of Odd or Even, screaming and wiggling their hands so deftly they could have put the marionettes in a puppet show to shame. In a far corner somebody was shouting 'Hey, c'mon over here and pour me a drink!' As he waved his flask around he must have noticed it was empty, and switched his demand to 'Hey, more saké! More saké!' All this yelling and commotion was just too much for me. And in the midst of it all one person sat there at a loss as to what to do with himself, eyes cast downward, sunk deep in thought. This was the Squash. The reason they were giving him this farewell banquet wasn't because they were sad to see him go. It was to give themselves an excuse to drink and have some fun. It was to make him feel miserable, sitting there alone, not knowing what to do with himself. If this was the best they could do by way of a farewell party, he would have been much better off if they hadn't bothered at all.

Eventually the rest of them started singing something or other in sloppy, raucous voices. One of the geisha came over to me with her shamisen at the ready and said 'You there, come on, give us a song,' but when I told her that I didn't sing and that she could sing something herself instead, she treated us to a ballad:

> Beating a drum and banging a gong
> With a chanchikirin and a dondokodon
> We'll go out looking for the little lost boy.
> And if you find the boy for you
> Beating a drum and banging a gong
> Well there's someone I want to look for too
> With a chanchikirin and a dondokodon . . .

Somehow she managed to get through all this on just two breaths, and then said 'Whew, I'm all worn out.' Too bad she didn't try something easier if this was going to wear her out.

Meanwhile the Hanger had come over and sat himself down next to her, saying 'Oh, poor Suzu-chan – just when it seemed like she'd finally found that someone she was looking for, he goes right home!' To this comment, which was delivered in the music-hall storyteller style he often affected, she sulkily replied 'I don't know what you're talking about.' The Hanger, totally oblivious, went right on, this time in an awful imitation of the narrator in a puppet drama: 'By chance did they meet, and yet . . .' The geisha squealed 'Stop it!' and slapped him on the knee; the Hanger-on beamed with delight. This was the same geisha that had said something to Redshirt before. Any man who could look so pleased when he got slapped by a geisha had to be a dolt. He wasn't finished with his antics, either: 'And now I'm going to dance "Kiinokuni" – Suzu-chan, play it for me please . . .'

On the other side of the room the old Chinese classics teacher was contorting his toothless mouth as he squeezed out a passage from one of the puppet plays: 'How can you say that, Denbei? The bond between you and me . . .' Having managed to get through that part safely, he turned to a geisha and asked 'Er, then what?' Old men do have a way of losing their memories. Another geisha had gotten hold of the science teacher: 'There's a brand new song that's going around,' she purred, 'and it goes like this. Let me play it for you, listen carefully now!' She proceeded to sing something about a girl who does her hair in the latest fashion, all tied up with a pretty white bow, rides around town on a bicycle, plays on a violin, and chatters away in broken English, telling everyone 'I am glad to see you.' 'Yes, that's a good one,' said the science teacher, obviously impressed ' – it's even got some English in it, doesn't it?'

Then it was the Porcupine's turn. In a ridiculously loud voice, he bellowed that he was going to perform a sword dance and commanded the geisha to accompany him on their shamisens. The ladies, stunned by the ferocity with which this order was issued, made no response. Unfazed, the Porcupine picked up a walking stick, marched off alone to the center of the room and, declaiming the classical lyrics 'Through the mists that veil a thousand peaks I tread my way,' revealed a long-hidden artistic talent. Meanwhile the Hanger, having danced his own way though 'Kiinokuni,' as well as some other favorites such as 'Kappore' and 'Tana no daruma,' had started parading around the room stripped down to his loincloth with a palm-leaf broom for a sword, singing 'Peace Talks with China Have Been Broken Off.' The man must have been out of his mind!

I was feeling tremendously sorry for the Squash, who was sitting stiffly through all this without undoing his formal kimono skirt, looking terribly uncomfortable. It was impossible to see why anybody should have to put up with sitting through his own farewell party in full formal dress while being subjected to the spectacle of a man prancing around in a loincloth, so I went over and urged him to leave with me, but he showed no signs of being willing to move. 'Since it's my farewell banquet,' he said, 'it wouldn't do for me to leave before the others, but please go right ahead yourself.'

'Don't worry about them,' I told him. 'If this is a farewell party, they should be *acting* like they were at a farewell party. Just look – they're madmen! Come on, let's go!' Finally I was able to overcome his reluctance, but just as we were on the point of escaping the Hanger charged up with his broom waving furiously and shouted 'What is the meaning of this! The guest of honor leaving first? It's an outrage! Peace talks with China! I won't let you go!' Holding his broom out sideways as a barrier, he blocked the way. I was already pretty riled up by this point, so I yelled 'Well, if peace talks with China have been broken off, you must be the Chinaman!' and let him have a healthy whack on the head. He just stood there in a kind of stupor for a couple of seconds, as if all the sense had suddenly been knocked out of him, then launched into an incoherent rant: 'Outrageous! To have laid a hand on me, sir, was most cruel! That I, Yoshikawa, should be subjected to bodily harm – how dare you? This, sir, is the final rupture of Sino-Japanese negotiations!' The Porcupine, noticing that some kind of fracas had erupted, broke off his own sword dance and came running up from behind. As soon as he

saw how badly the situation was deteriorating he grabbed the
Hanger by the neck and jerked him away. 'Sino-Japanese . . .
Ouch! That hurts!! Such violence!' The Hanger tried to wriggle
free but was wrenched sideways and fell to the floor with a
resounding thump. I don't know what happened after that. I
walked part of the way back together with the Squash before
saying goodbye; by the time I got home it was past eleven.

10

The war was over and classes were cancelled on account of the victory celebration. A ceremony was going to be held at the parade ground in town; the students would be marching in the procession, with the Badger leading the way. I was also to participate as a member of the faculty. When we got to town there were Japanese flags flying all over the place; the scene was so dazzling it made your head swim. The student body numbered eight hundred. According to the plan, the physical education teacher would organize them into neat ranks and files, arranged by classes, with one or two teachers marching along as supervisors in the gaps between one class and the next. An exceedingly well thought out plan to be sure, but the reality turned out to be exceedingly messy. Not only were the students still children, they were cheeky ones into the bargain, and naturally they would have considered it a disgrace if they failed to throw a monkey wrench into the proceedings. No matter how many teachers were there to try and keep them in line it was a lost cause. First they would break into a soldiers' marching song, even though nobody had directed them to do it; then they'd send up a series of ragged battle cries as if they were a bunch of renegade samurai swaggering around the town. The intervals between the marching songs and the yells were filled with noisy chatter. You'd think they'd be able to walk in a straight line without saying anything, but Japanese people are born mouth first, so all our scolding just fell on deaf ears. And it wasn't just ordinary chatter, either: they were busy bad-mouthing their teachers, really low-grade stuff. I had imagined that once I'd forced an apology out of the students after the

night-duty incident things would probably settle down. In the
event, though, things turned out very differently. As my old
landlady might have put it, I'd been good and hoodwinked. The
students had apologized, all right, but it wasn't because they
sincerely regretted what they'd done. The Principal had ordered
them to do it, so they came to me and bowed their heads, but it
was only an empty gesture. Just like those shopkeepers who
bow their heads to you obsequiously while they go right on
cheating you, these kids might apologize, but there was no way
they'd ever stop making trouble. When you stop and think
about it, maybe the whole human race is made up of people like
those students. So anybody who takes other people at their
word and pardons them when they apologize for something or
beg for forgiveness deserves to be called a fool for being too
honest. If people's apologies aren't the real thing, you might as
well think of their forgiveness as not being the real thing either.
To get a genuine apology from somebody, you're going to have
to keep beating them until their regret is genuine too.

As I walked along between the class groups, I could hear
comments about tempura this and dumplings that, over and
over again. With so many kids, it was impossible to pick out the
ones who were saying all this. Of course, even if I could, they
would just claim that they hadn't said anything of the kind, and
that I was hearing things because I had a warped mind or was
having a nervous breakdown or some other such nonsense. This
vile attitude of theirs was an ingrained habit that had been
nurtured in their region since feudal times, so no matter how
hard you tried to persuade them or browbeat them, there was
no cure for it. After a year in a place like this, even somebody
untainted like me might find himself having to do as the locals
do and end up the same way. There was no way that I was going
to let anybody throw mud in my face and then get out of taking
responsibility for it with some slick kind of dodge. Was I any
less of a person than they were? Even if they were schoolboys,
even if they were just kids, they were already bigger than I was.
That being the case, it wouldn't be right if I didn't manage to make
them pay with some kind of punishment. But if I tried to go
after them by one of the usual methods, they were sure to come

right back after me. If I told them that they'd done something wrong and were only getting what they deserved, they'd have their excuses all ready beforehand and eloquently proclaim their innocence. Not only that, they'd also manage to create the impression that *they* were actually the fine, upstanding ones and go on to attack me for having picked on them. Since my whole point was to exact some payback, there would be no point to it unless their misconduct was established. In other words, if they could attack me and then get everybody to believe that I was the one who had started the fight, they'd have me over a barrel. But then if I let them have their way and played the part of an easygoing, spineless chump, it would only make them that much bolder – or, to look at things on a grander scale, it wouldn't help make the world a better place. So, basically, this meant that I had no choice but to adopt the tactics of my opponents and find a way to get retribution without being tripped up in the process. That would be the end for me as a self-respecting Edokko. But if I was going to have to put up with a year of this kind of treatment, well, I'm human too, so whether it meant throwing away my self-respect or whatever, that's the way I'd have to do it if I was ever going to settle the score. The only way out of this mess was to go back to Tokyo and rejoin Kiyo right away. Staying on in a boondock like this was like pushing myself toward my own downfall. Even taking a job delivering newspapers would have to be better than that.

As I dragged myself along keeping my place in the procession with these thoughts running through my head, I suddenly became aware of some kind of commotion at the head of the column. At the exact same moment, the lines of marchers came to a sudden halt. Wondering what was going on, I slipped out past the right end of the line and surveyed the scene. Up ahead where the road turned the corner from Otemachi into Yakushimachi, the marchers had stopped in their tracks. I could see a lot of jostling going on: some of the students were busy trying to shove people out of the way; others were getting shoved back themselves. The physical education teacher came running back toward us, hoarsely calling for everyone to stay calm. When I asked him what was going on, he reported that our students had bumped into a column of students from the local normal school up at the corner.

According to what I was told, the students in middle schools and normal schools in any provincial town fight like cats and dogs. I don't know why this is, but it does seem as if they rub each other the wrong way, and any little thing can touch off a fight. Probably they get so bored living in these little country towns that they just do it to help pass the time. Now, I like a good fight myself, so when I heard that a brawl had broken out I ran up to see what was going on. I could hear the kids at the front shouting 'Out of our way, you local-tax-school losers!' Shouts of 'Push 'em back! Push 'em back!' came welling up from behind. Just as I was getting close to the intersection, slipping past the knots of students that were blocking my way, the order 'Forward march!' was issued in a strong, sharp voice, and the normal school students calmly began moving forward. The question of who would go first, which had been the point of contention in the melee, had obviously been settled, and the middle school had given way. The normal school, I was told, qualified as the higher-ranking institution.

The victory celebration was a very simple ceremony. The local brigade commander read a congratulatory message, and then the Governor read one; the crowd shouted out a couple of ceremonial banzais, and that was all. They said that there would be an entertainment program in the afternoon, so in the meantime I went home and started writing a letter to Kiyo, which had been on my mind ever since I'd read hers. She had asked me to write her more details about my life here, so I would have to try to give her as thorough an account as possible. When I actually took out some paper and sat down to write, though, there was so much to tell her that I had no idea where to begin. I could write about this, but it would be a bother; I could write about that, but it would be a bore. I racked my brains trying to come up with something that I could get down on paper smoothly without too much aggravation and that would be of interest to her, but I couldn't think of any topics that filled the bill. I rubbed my inkstone, dipped the tip of my brush in the ink, and stared at the blank sheet of paper; then I stared at the paper, wet my brush, and rubbed the inkstone again. After repeating this same routine over and over, in the same way, I finally arrived at the conclusion that there was no way I could compose a letter, and put away my inkstone. What a lot of bother it is to write a letter! It would have been a lot simpler just to go to Tokyo and tell her everything in person. It wasn't as if I didn't care about how worried Kiyo was, but writing her the kind of letter she wanted would be more excruciating than going on a three-week fast.

I flung my brush and paper aside, sprawled out on the floor, and lay there gazing out at the garden with my head resting on my arm. I was still concerned about Kiyo. It occurred to me that even though we were separated by such a great distance now, as long as I continued to worry about how she was getting on, she would surely realize my true feelings. And as long as she was aware of them, there was no need for me to send anything like a letter. If I didn't send one she'd probably assume that everything was all right. You could do without sending a letter until something really big happened – a death, say, or an illness.

The garden was a level patch of ground about twenty feet square, with nothing special in the way of plantings. There was a single mandarin orange tree, so tall that its top rose above the garden wall and served as a kind of landmark for the house. I always liked to gaze at this tree when I came home. For someone who had never been out of Tokyo before, the sight of the fruit hanging on the tree was a truly novel one. As they ripened, the green oranges would no doubt be turning to a golden color; that, I was sure, would be beautiful to see. Some of them were starting to change color already. According to the landlady, they were exceptionally juicy and delicious. She'd told me that I could help myself when they were ready to eat, and I was already looking forward to the time when I'd be able to enjoy a few each day. In another three weeks there ought to be plenty of them; surely, I thought, I wouldn't be leaving here before then.

While I was lying there thinking about those oranges, the Porcupine suddenly turned up. Today being the day of the victory celebration, he said, he'd decided that the two of us ought to indulge in a little feast, so he had gone out and bought some beef; with this, he pulled a package wrapped in a bamboo sheath out of the sleeve of his kimono and tossed it on the floor beside me. Since I was still being subjected to the sweet potato and tofu treatment at home, and the noodle shop and dumpling shop had been placed strictly off limits as well, this was a welcome treat indeed. I went off to borrow a pan and some sugar from the landlady, and we started cooking right away.

As the Porcupine was stuffing his face with beef, he asked me if I knew that Redshirt was a regular customer of a certain geisha. 'Of course I do,' I said. 'She's one of the ones that were at the farewell banquet, right?' Yes, that was her, he replied, and complimented me for having been sharp enough to figure it out when he himself hadn't gotten wind of it until just now.

'Just look at the guy,' he said. 'Every other word that comes out of his mouth is "character" or "spiritual amusements" – and then he goes and takes up with some geisha on the sly. He makes me sick. It wouldn't be so bad if he was ready to accept what other people do for fun, but no – all you have to do is step into a noodle shop or a dumpling shop and he has the Principal warn you about setting a bad example . . .'

'Yeah,' I told him, 'I guess that hiring a geisha is a spiritual amusement as far as that joker's concerned, but tempura and dumplings are materialistic ones. If it's so spiritual, why doesn't he flaunt it a little more? How could he have pulled a stunt like that – getting up and running away as soon as he sees that geisha of his coming in the room? He thinks he can keep pulling the wool over our eyes forever. That's what really gets me. And then when somebody attacks him he just says "I don't know what you're talking about,' or tries to bamboozle you by spouting some nonsense about Russian literature, or haiku being the big brother of modern poetry. He's not even a man at all, he's just a big sissy. He must be a reincarnation of one of those old-time palace lady's maids that specialized in all kinds of intrigue. Or maybe his old man was one of those boys that plied their trade in the shadows over by the shrine in Yushima . . .'

'Huh? Boys in the shadows in Yushima?'

'Well, they weren't exactly what you'd call manly, if you know what I mean . . . Hey, that piece isn't cooked yet, don't eat it or you'll end up with a tapeworm!'

'Really? Oh, it's probably all right. Anyway, they say that Redshirt sneaks out to the hot spring to see that geisha at a house called Kado-ya.'

'Kado-ya? You mean that inn?'

'It's an inn, but it also has a restaurant. So the best way to put him on the spot would be to catch him in the act when he's going in there with the geisha and give him a good tongue-lashing.'

'Catch him in the act? How? In a stakeout?'

'That's right. You know the inn called Masu-ya that's right across from Kado-ya? Well, I can rent one of the second-floor rooms on the front side, poke a little hole in one of the paper screens, and keep a lookout.'

'Do you think he'll actually come along while you're looking?'

'I think so. Of course, one night won't be enough. I'll have to be ready to give it a good two weeks or so.'

'That'll be exhausting! I remember when my old man died, I stayed up with him every night for a week, and when it was all over I felt like I was in a daze. It really took a lot out of me.'

'A little fatigue won't hurt me. It wouldn't be doing Japan any favors to let a rogue like him keep running loose; I'm going to make myself an agent of divine retribution.'

'Sounds great! If you do go through with it I'll help you out. Are you going to start watching tonight?'

'Not tonight. I haven't talked to the people at Masu-ya yet.'

'Well, when do you plan to start, then?'

'Soon enough. Anyway I'll let you know, so I hope you'll lend a hand when the time comes.'

'Fine, I'll be ready to help any time. I'm not much good at hatching schemes, but when it comes to a fight I'm pretty handy.'

While the Porcupine and I were working out the details of the scheme, the landlady appeared at the door. 'Mr Hotta,' she announced, 'one of the boys from the school is here and he'd like to talk to you, na moshi. He says that he went to your home but since you were out he thought you might be here and came over to see, na moshi.' She knelt politely in the doorway, awaiting the Porcupine's reply. 'All right,' he said, and went out to the front entrance. When he came back he reported that the student had come to invite him to go along to the entertainment portion of the victory celebration. After hearing that there was going to be a troupe of dancers from Kōchi doing some kind of special dance that you hardly ever get a chance to see, he was all for going and urged me to go too. I had seen plenty of dances in Tokyo; there was a big festival every year at the local shrine with people dancing on floats that were pulled around the neighborhood, so I knew about the Salt Gatherers' Dance and all the rest. I had no interest in seeing a bunch of hicks from Kōchi making fools of themselves, but since the Porcupine had made a point of inviting me I figured that I might as well go anyway. The boy who had come to invite him, it turned out, was none other than that brother of Redshirt's. Kind of odd that it should be him, of all people!

The vast stretch of sky above the parade ground had come alive with countless pennants and banners fluttering from the tips of long poles that had been set up all over the place, which reminded me of the scene at the sumo tournament at Ekō-in or the big Buddhist memorial services at the Honmon Temple in Tokyo. There were also flags flying on a network of ropes which had been strung up overhead, so many of them that it seemed as if they must have borrowed one from every country in the world. At the eastern corner a temporary stage had been set up for that Kōchi dance, whatever it was. About sixty yards to the right of the stage there was an exhibition of flower arrangements, surrounded by screens made of reed blinds. Everybody was oohing and aahing at these, but it was completely worthless as far as I was concerned. If you're going to get so excited about a bunch of twisted shrubs or bamboo, you might as well feel proud about having a hunchbacked lover or a lame husband while you're at it.

On the opposite side of the grounds from the stage they were busy shooting off fireworks. As one of these burst it released a balloon with the words NIPPON BANZAI printed on it, which drifted over the pine trees by the castle and then fell inside the barracks compound. Next there was a popping sound and a black dumpling arched across the autumn sky and then burst open right above my head. Streamers of bluish smoke shot out

like the ribs of a parasol and lazily melted away in the air. Then
came another balloon. This one was red and said ARMY AND
NAVY BANZAI in white letters. Tossed about by the wind, it
floated off over the hot spring toward Aioi village. Maybe it
came back to earth inside the grounds of the goddess of mercy's
temple.

The crowd was much bigger now than it had been for the
morning ceremony. Looking at the swarming throng, I had to
marvel that even a country town could be so full of people. Most
of them didn't look particularly clever, but only a fool could
take such sheer numbers of people lightly. By and by, that something-or-other dance from Kōchi, which was supposed to be so
impressive, got under way. I had figured that it would be an
ordinary dance, something along the lines of the Fujima or one
of the other usual styles, but my guess was way off.

Up on the stage were three rows of ten men each, all of them
with impressive-looking headbands knotted at the back and
kimono skirts tied in with cords at the knees. What really
shocked me, though, was that they were all carrying naked
swords. There was only about a foot and a half of space between
the rows, and no more than that much distance between the
dancers in each row. A single dancer stood off by himself at the
edge of the stage. This loner was also wearing a kimono skirt,
but he hadn't invested in a headband, and instead of carrying a
sword he had a drum – the same kind they use in the Chinese
lion dance – hanging from a strap around his neck. He got things
started with a sluggish shout of 'Yaah! Haah!' and a strange
chant accompanied by a ba-da-boom, ba-da-boom rhythm on
the drum. The tune was eerie, not like anything else I had ever
heard; if you imagine something that sounded like a cross
between a comical New Year's minstrel song and a mournful
Buddhist pilgrim's chant, you wouldn't be too far off.

The song went along at an extremely loose, relaxed pace, as
shapeless as a blob of jelly on a summer day, but at least the
drummer was marking off each phrase in the flow of sound
with a ba-da-boom, so you could pick up some kind of a rhythm.
The dancers were flashing their swords in time to this rhythm,
with such speed and precision that just watching them was

enough to make you break out in a cold sweat. Only a foot and a half away on each side, as well as behind, was a live human being – and each of them was twirling his own naked sword around in exactly the same way, so unless they all moved with just the right timing somebody would end up getting hurt by one of his fellow dancers. It wouldn't have been so dangerous if they were simply standing in place while they waved their swords up and down and backward and forward, but all thirty of them also had to keep in step as they stamped their feet and turned to the side or wheeled around full circle or dipped their knees at the same time. If the dancer next to you was just a second too fast, or a second too slow, your nose might come flying right off – or you might slice off your neighbor's head. Each sword was swinging freely within its own space, but that space was limited to a column about eighteen inches square, and it had to be wielded in the exact same direction at the exact same speed as the swords in front and behind and to the right and left. This was a revelation – ordinary dances like the Salt Gatherers and the Gateway Door simply couldn't compare. It takes tremendous skill, I was told; learning the technique of synchronizing your movements like that was no easy thing. People said that the hardest job of all, though, was being in charge of the funny song and the ba-da-boom. Everything that the thirty dancers did – their footwork, the way they waved their swords and twisted their hips – it all depended entirely on one thing, the rhythm set by this ba-da-boom man. Strangely enough this guy appeared to be the most relaxed person on the stage, belting out his yaahs and haahs whenever he pleased, but actually it was a tremendously heavy responsibility and he had to give it everything he'd got.

As the Porcupine and I were standing there awestruck, totally absorbed in the performance, a huge roar suddenly went up about fifty yards away. The throngs of people who had been calmly circulating among the various attractions now broke off toward the sides in massive waves. No sooner had we heard somebody yell 'It's a fight! It's a fight!' than Redshirt's little brother came cutting through the forest of sleeves and shouted 'They're fighting again, sir! The middle school students are taking their revenge on the normal school for this morning – they've just started a battle to settle things once and for all! You'd better come right away!' Then he melted back into the crowd.

'What, they're at it again? Nothing but trouble, those brats! Enough is enough!' The Porcupine was off in a flash, dodging through the waves of people that were fleeing the scene. He must have decided that he couldn't just stand idly by and let the melee go on. I had no intention of running away either, of course, and I followed close on his heels. By the time we got to the spot, the fight was already going full blast. There must have been about fifty or sixty students from the normal school, and a group about a third bigger from the middle school. The normal school boys were still in their uniforms, but most of the kids from the middle school had changed into kimono after the ceremony so it was easy to tell the two sides apart. But since they were all mixed in together, coming to grips and breaking off in ever-changing patterns, I had no idea how to go about getting them separated, or where to start. The Porcupine stood there for a couple of seconds surveying the fracas with an oh-no kind of look, but then turned to me and said 'No choice now. We wouldn't want the police to see this. Let's get in there and break it up!' Without bothering to reply, I plunged right in at the point where the fighting looked fiercest. 'Stop, stop! You're a disgrace to your school! Cut it out, I tell you!!' Hollering at the top of my lungs, I tried to weave along what seemed to be the front line, but it was no easy feat. By the time I had worked my way a couple of yards in, I was hopelessly stuck. Right in front of me one of the bigger normal school kids was grappling with a middle school kid of fifteen or sixteen. 'When I say stop, I mean stop!' I yelled, and grabbed the normal school kid by the shoulder to try and tear him away. At the same moment, though, somebody tripped me from below. Caught off balance, I lost my grip on the kid's shoulder and tumbled to one side. Somebody jumped on my back with a pair of hard shoes. I sprang back up on my hands and knees, throwing the guy off and sending him bouncing down to the right. Back on my feet, I could see the Porcupine about twenty feet away, hemmed in by swarms of students, shouting 'Stop it! Stop this fighting right now!!' as his big body was being pushed to and fro in the swirling mob. 'Hey! It's no use!' I yelled, but there was no response. Maybe he couldn't hear.

All of a sudden a rock came whizzing in and hit me smack on the cheekbone, followed right away by somebody coming up from behind and whacking me across the back with a stick. I could hear a voice screaming 'Hit him! Hit him! What's a teacher doing getting mixed up in this?' Somebody else chimed in: 'There are two of them, a big guy and a little one. Pelt 'em with rocks!' 'You stupid hicks,' I bellowed. 'Who the hell do you think you are?' Then I wound up and gave a normal school student standing nearby a sock in the face. Another rock came whistling in; this one brushed right past the side of my head and flew off behind me. I couldn't see what had become of the Porcupine. No choice now. When I first waded in I was trying to break up the fight, but now that I was getting whacked and having rocks thrown at me, I'd be damned if I was going to cut and run like some kind of ninny. 'Who do you think you're dealing with? I may be a little guy, but I learned my stuff in Tokyo, where the real fighters come from!' With that battle cry I charged in like a madman, bashing people and getting bashed back, until I heard somebody shout 'Police! It's the police! Let's get out of here!' Up to this point it had been so hard to move in the crush of bodies that I felt like I was wading in some kind of sticky paste, but all of a sudden things eased up and before I knew it everybody, friend and foe alike, was rushing for the exits. They may have been hicks, but when it came to beating a retreat they were real experts. Even a professional like General Kuropatkin could have learned a thing or two from this crew.

Wondering what had happened to the Porcupine, I looked around and saw him up ahead wiping his nose, his kimono jacket with his family crest embroidered on it in shreds. Somebody had punched him in the nose, he told me, and it had been bleeding heavily. Now it was bright red and all swollen, a really horrible sight. I was in a less formal kimono, so even though it was splattered with mud it wasn't as much of a loss as the Porcupine's jacket. I had an awful stinging pain in my cheek, though, and according to the Porcupine it was bleeding quite a bit.

A force of fifteen or sixteen policemen had arrived on the

scene, but since the students had taken off in the opposite direction, the only people who got caught were the Porcupine and me. After we identified ourselves and gave them a full account of the incident, they told us that we'd better go down to the police station. There we gave a deposition in the presence of the chief; then we headed home.

When I woke up the next morning, my whole body ached unbearably; it must have been because I'd been out of practice as a fighter for too long. As I lay there in bed, thinking to myself that I couldn't do much boasting about my fighting abilities now, the landlady brought in the *Shikoku News* and left it by my pillow. I didn't even really feel up to taking a look at a paper, but, I thought to myself, I wouldn't be much of a man if I let a little thing like this get the better of me, so I forced myself over onto my stomach and started reading. When I turned to the second page, I was flabbergasted. There was an article on last night's fight, but that was no surprise. The real shocker was the report that 'two teachers from the middle school, a certain Mr Hotta and a certain impertinent party who had recently been hired from Tokyo, not only precipitated the altercation by inciting the innocent students but also assumed direction of the fray and even went so far as to engage in acts of unprovoked and unrestrained violence against the normal school students.' It went on to provide the following commentary:

Our prefectural middle school's reputation for superior quality and model conduct has long made it the object of envy throughout the land, but the thoughtless acts of this puerile twosome have blemished the good name of our school and brought dishonor upon the entire community. Under these circumstances, we feel it our duty to call the responsible parties to account with all due vigor. We are confident, however, that before we take matters into our own hands the competent authorities will adopt appropriate punitive measures with regard to the two malefactors

and ensure that they will never again be afforded the opportunity
to participate in educational activities.

Every single letter of this diatribe had been printed with a little
black dot next to it for emphasis, as if they had been trying to
give the page acupuncture treatment. With a cry of 'Eat shit!' I
sprang out of bed. Incredibly, as soon as I did so, the awful pain
that I'd been feeling in every joint of my body suddenly eased
so much that it already seemed to be a thing of the past.

I crumpled the newspaper into a ball and flung it out into the
garden. I still felt so furious, though, that I went out and picked
it up again and then stuffed it down the toilet. Newspapers print
all kinds of outrageous lies. If you've ever wondered where to
find the biggest blowhards in the world, well, a newspaper is the
place. Here they were giving people their version of a story that
I should have been giving myself. And then to call me 'a certain
impertinent party who had recently been hired from Tokyo' –
who the hell did they think they were? Is there anybody in the
world who goes by the name of 'a certain party,' impertinent or
otherwise? Use your head – no matter what else you could say
about me, at least I have a perfectly good name, and if you want
to see it, I'll be glad to show you my complete family tree, going
all the way back to Minamoto no Mitsunaka . . .

As I was washing my face, I suddenly felt a pain in my cheek.
I asked the landlady to lend me a mirror, and when she brought
it, she asked if I had read the paper yet. I told her that I had, and
then I'd stuffed it down the toilet, so if she wanted it she'd have
to fish it out herself. Astonished, she walked off. When I looked
at my face in the mirror, the bruises from last night were still
there. No matter what else you could say about my face, it
matters a lot to me; to end up with that face covered in bruises
and on top of that to be reduced to the level of a nameless 'certain
impertinent party' – it was all too much.

If I'd let that newspaper intimidate me and hid out at home
all day I'd never have been able to live it down, so as soon as I
finished breakfast I dashed out the door and got to school before
anybody else. As the other teachers arrived, each of them broke
into a smile when they saw my face. What was so funny, I thought

to myself – it's not as if it was any of you guys that created this face for me in the first place. By and by the Hanger-on turned up. 'That was quite an exploit last night – those bruises, I suppose, are your badges of honor?' he sneered. Maybe this was his way of getting back at me for the beating he took at the farewell party. 'Never mind about me,' I told him, 'you just run along and lick your brush,' to which he replied 'Well, now, I do beg you pardon, but then it must be terribly painful, I fear.' 'Painful or not, it's my face,' I hollered. 'What business is it of yours?' He went and sat down at his desk, but he kept staring at me and smirking as he whispered something to the history teacher sitting next to him.

The Porcupine arrived before long, too. His nose was purple and swollen and looked like it would start oozing pus if you stuck it with something. Maybe it was just vanity on my part, but I couldn't help thinking that he seemed to have taken a much worse beating than I had. The two of us had our desks right next to each other; not only did we look like two sorry peas in a pod, but unfortunately our desks faced straight toward the faculty room door. That pair of faces had to be a pretty wondrous sight. Any time one of the other teachers had nothing better to do, his gaze would drift in our direction. 'How awful!' was what they all said, but I'm sure they were really thinking 'What a pair of idiots!' If not, why would they all be whispering and giggling the way they were? When I walked into my classroom, I was greeted with a round of applause, plus two or three banzais. Whether this was a display of high spirits or they were just being wise guys was hard to tell. Amid all the fuss, the one person who acted just the same as usual was Redshirt. 'What a terrible mishap,' he said when he came over to us, and then offered what amounted to a semi-apology: 'I feel so sorry for both of you. I've discussed that article in the newspaper with the Principal, and we've made an official request for a retraction, so there's nothing to worry about. Since the whole affair started with my own brother's invitation to Mr Hotta, I can't tell you how badly I feel about it. At any rate I'm absolutely determined to do whatever I can to make things right, so I hope you won't hold this against me.' During the third period the Principal emerged from his office and commented, with a somewhat worried look, that the newspaper article had certainly created a problem, and he hoped that the consequences would not be too drastic. Personally, I wasn't worried in the least. If they wanted to dismiss me over this, all I had to do was turn in my resignation first. But for me to give in when I hadn't done anything wrong would just make those blowhards at the newspaper feel even more pleased with themselves. The right thing to do, I was sure, was for me to dig in and stay at my post, and force the newspaper to print a retraction. I'd even been thinking about stopping in at the newspaper office on my way home to state my case, but once I heard that the school had already asked them to withdraw their claims, I decided not to do it.

In between classes and other business the Porcupine and I managed to give the Principal and Redshirt a fairly complete picture of the way things had really happened. They both sounded sympathetic, and took the view that the people at the newspaper must have made a point of printing such a story because they bore some kind of grudge against the school. Redshirt then went around the faculty room talking to each of our colleagues in turn, defending our conduct and making it sound like it had all been his fault, since his brother was the one who asked the Porcupine to attend in the first place. Everybody agreed that the newspaper was the guilty party; it was inexcusable, and the two of us were the real victims of the incident.

As I was leaving for the day, the Porcupine pulled me aside and warned me that there was something fishy going on with Redshirt; if we didn't watch out, he added, we could be in for it. 'I know, he's been fishy all along,' I replied, 'he didn't just get that way overnight.' According to the Porcupine, though, I was missing the point: making sure that we were invited to the celebration and then getting us mixed up in the fight was all part of a scheme. That was something I hadn't thought about before, but now it was perfectly clear. The Porcupine might have looked like a ruffian all right, but you had to admire the way he used his head.

'First he gets us into the fight, then he goes straight to the newspaper and gets them to write that story. The man's a real snake, I tell you.'

'So the article was his work, too? Incredible! But would the newspaper people really just go along with whatever he told them?'

'Why not? Nothing to it if he's got a friend on the staff.'

'But does he?'

'Even if he doesn't, nothing to it. They'll print anything, any kind of lie, as long as you look like you know what you're talking about and tell it with a straight face.'

'This is terrible! If it was all a trap that Redshirt set for us, it could end up getting us fired!'

'If things go wrong, it could be all over for us.'

'Well, if that's the case, I'll just turn in my resignation tomorrow and go back to Tokyo. I wouldn't stay in this dump if they begged me . . .'

'That wouldn't be a problem as far as Redshirt's concerned.'

'Hmm, true enough. What could we do that *would* be a problem?'

'Rogues like him are always careful not to leave any tracks no matter what they're up to, so he won't be easy to catch.'

'What a bind. We'd just end up looking like we were making false accusations. No fun at all! Isn't there any justice in this world?'

'Anyway, let's wait a couple of days and see what happens. Then if worst comes to worst, we'll just have to catch him at the hot spring, I guess.'

'And not try to do anything about the newspaper?'

'That's right. We'll go on the attack ourselves and hit him in his weak spot instead.'

'Sounds good. I'm hopeless when it comes to strategy, so I'll leave that all up to you. But whenever you need me, I'll be ready for anything.'

With that, the Porcupine and I went our own ways. If Redshirt had really done what the Porcupine suspected he had, he was definitely a first-class scoundrel. Not the kind of guy you could hope to prevail over in a battle of wits. Nothing but brute force would do. It's no wonder wars keep breaking out all over the world. Even on the individual level, when you come right down to it, brute force is what counts.

I could hardly wait for the newspaper to appear the next morning, but when it did, there was nothing in it in the way of a retraction, let alone a more accurate account of the incident. When I asked the Badger about it at school, he said that there would probably be something appearing the following day. And there was – a retraction, printed in the smallest possible type. No attempt to print a corrected version, of course. I tried taking my case to him again, but this time he said that there was no further recourse to be had. Behind that badger face of his and all that preening in his frock coat, this Principal had surprisingly little clout. He couldn't even get a country newspaper to apologize for printing an article that was full of lies! This was too much for me to take, so I announced that I would go and lodge a protest with the editor myself, but the Badger, in tones that would have been better suited to a Buddhist priest sermonizing on the spirit of renunciation, told me that this wouldn't do. 'If you complain to them, they'll just print another article raking you over the coals. The fact is, when they write something about you in the paper there isn't a thing you can do about it, regardless of whether it's true or false. You just have to live with it.' If that's really the way things are, we'd all be a lot better off if the newspapers were driven out of business, and the sooner the better. Getting written about in a newspaper is like getting bitten by a snapping turtle – once it latches onto you, it won't let go. This is what I now realized, thanks to my talk with the Badger.

One afternoon about three days later, the Porcupine paid me a visit. Seething with indignation, he announced that the time had finally come and he was going to put his plan into action. In that case, I said, I was ready to join him right away in the league of the righteous, but the Porcupine shook his head and advised me to stay out of it. When I asked him why, he answered by asking me whether I had been called in by the Principal and ordered to submit a letter of resignation. No, I said, and how about you? He then reported that earlier that day he had been informed, in the Principal's office, that although it was indeed regrettable, due to unavoidable circumstances the school would be obliged to ask him to relinquish his position.

'What kind of justice is that?' I said. 'That Badger must have been beating his chest so hard that he knocked himself senseless. The two of us went to the victory celebration together. And we watched those dancers flash their swords together, didn't we? And we tried to stop that fight together, didn't we? If he's asking you to resign, he should ask me, too. It's only fair. Why do these country schools have to be so damned unreasonable? It's driving me crazy!'

'Redshirt's behind the whole thing. After everything that's gone on up till now there isn't enough room in this school for both of us, but he figures that he can keep you on because you won't be any threat to him.'

'It's not big enough for Redshirt and me, either. He's got some nerve thinking I'm not a threat.'

'Well, he must think that you're so simple-minded he can always keep you around and bamboozle you any time he needs to.'

'That's even worse! There's no conceivable way this school could be big enough for him and me!'

'And besides, have you noticed that the replacement they hired for Koga hasn't arrived yet for some reason? If they got rid of both of us now, they wouldn't have enough people to cover all of the classes, so . . .'

'So they think they can just keep me around as a fill-in, huh? Damn them! No way I'll let them get away with that!'

When I went to school the next morning I headed straight to the Principal's office.

'I want to know why you didn't ask for my resignation.'

'What?' The Badger looked stunned.

'What kind of sense does it make to ask Hotta to resign, but not me?'

'The school does have its reasons . . .'

'Well, those reasons are all wrong. If I don't have to resign, then there shouldn't be any need for Hotta to, either.'

'It's all rather difficult to explain, but . . . Hotta's leaving is an unavoidable circumstance, but I see no need for you to follow suit.'

Leave it to the sly old Badger to sit there cool as a cucumber while he spouted this load of hogwash. There was nothing else I could do now, so I let him have it.

'Well, in that case, I'm resigning too. You may think that if you make Hotta quit I'll just take it in my stride and stay on, but I couldn't let him down like that.'

'That won't do. If you left along with Hotta, the school would have nobody to teach the math classes.'

'That's your problem, not mine.'

'You mustn't be so selfish. You need to give a little thought to the good of the school – and besides, if you leave after less than a month on the job, how is it going to look on your record? You'd better think a little more about that, too.'

'Who cares about my record? Doing what's right is more important.'

'Well, I have to agree with that – in fact, I have to agree with everything you've said. But please give a little consideration to what *I* have to say. If you insist on resigning, well, so be it, but I hope that you'll at least stay on long enough for us to find somebody else. Anyway, please go home and think it over one more time.'

There was nothing to think over – my reason for quitting was as clear as daylight – but watching the Badger's face go pale and then bright red and then back again I couldn't help feeling sorry for him, so I said I'd try thinking it over and took my leave. I didn't even bother talking to Redshirt. If we were going to go after him at all, we might as well hit him with everything we had.

When I filled the Porcupine in on my parley with the Principal, he said yes, that was pretty much what he expected the man would say, and added that I might as well hold off on resigning until the time was ripe, so that was what I did. It seemed that he was actually a good deal shrewder than I was, so I was ready to leave all the decisions to him.

The Porcupine finally handed in his resignation, bid his formal farewell to the assembled faculty, and took a room in the Minato-ya down by the harbor; but without letting anybody get wind of it he made his way back to the hot spring and holed up in a second-floor room on the front side of Masu-ya, poked a peep-hole in the paper window, and started keeping watch. I was probably the only one who knew what he was doing. If Redshirt was going to slip in across the street, it would have to be at night.

And it would have to be sometime after nine, since he might be noticed by somebody, even a student, if he came earlier in the evening. For the first two nights I kept lookout with the Porcupine until eleven, but there was no sign of him. The third night we watched until half past ten – still nothing doing. Nothing makes you feel more foolish than walking back home in the middle of the night after another night of coming up empty-handed. By the fourth or fifth night old Mrs Hagino was starting to get concerned, and she warned me that it wasn't a good thing for a married man to be spending his nights out on the town. Of course her idea of being out on the town had nothing to do with what I was actually up to – serving as an agent of divine retribution. Anyway, going back and forth like that for a full week without having anything to show for our stakeout was no fun. Being the impulsive type, I have no problem with staying up all night working when I'm fired up about something, but the other side of the coin is that I can never manage to keep it up for very long. Even as an agent of the Divine Retribution League, it was no different. By the sixth night I was getting a little tired of it; by the seventh I was thinking about calling it quits. This is where the Porcupine showed just how tenacious he was. From early in the evening all the way past midnight he kept his eye glued to that peephole and focused right on the gaslit doorway of the Kado-ya across the street. What really amazed me, though, was that when I went to visit him he would show me a detailed list of how many people had gone into Kado-ya that day, how many of them were spending the night there, how many were women, and other such statistics. When I'd say, 'Looks like he isn't coming, doesn't it?' there were times when he'd fold his arms, sigh a little, and reply 'Well, I'm sure he'll turn up sooner or later, but . . .' Poor fellow! If Redshirt didn't put in an appearance, the Porcupine's divine mission could never be carried out.

On the eighth night I left my place around seven, had a nice leisurely dip at the hot spring, and then picked up eight eggs from a shop to fortify myself against my old landlady's sweet potato offensive. With four of the eggs stuck in each sleeve, my usual red towel slung over my shoulder, and my hands buried inside the front of my kimono, I went up the stairway to the second floor of Masu-ya. When I slid open the Porcupine's door, I could sense right away that things were looking up; that fierce guardian-god-Idaten face of his had suddenly regained its old glow. Up until then he had seemed a little glum; just being around him was enough to make me feel kind of depressed myself. Once I saw his expression that night my own spirits began to rise too, and before he even had a chance to tell me anything I let out a whoop of joy.

'Around half past seven tonight that geisha Kosuzu went in the door.'

'With Redshirt?'

'Well, no.'

'Well, then, it's no good, is it?'

'But there was another geisha with her . . . I just have a good feeling about this.'

'How come?'

'How come? Well, you know what a sly fox he is. He might be sending the two geisha in first and planning to slip in later himself.'

'Hmm, could be. It's past nine already, isn't it?'

He pulled his nickel-plated pocket watch out from underneath his sash. 'Just twelve past nine. Hey, better put out the lamp – if he sees two crew-cut silhouettes up here it might make him wonder. Foxes are very suspicious, you know.'

I blew out the lamp, which was sitting on a lacquer table. The paper window was still lit faintly by the starry sky. The moon wasn't up yet. The Porcupine and I kept our faces pressed against the window and held our breath. We could hear the chime of the wall clock downstairs as it struck nine thirty.

'I wonder if he's really coming tonight. If he doesn't, I give up.'

'I'm staying right here till my money runs out.'

'How much have you got?'

'So far I've given them five sixty for eight nights. I'm paying by the night so I can take off any time.'

'Good thinking. I'll bet the inn people are puzzled.'

'They don't mind. The real problem is I can never let up.'

'But you can sleep during the day, can't you?'

'I do, but I can't go out at all. Being stuck in here all day is driving me crazy.'

'Divine retribution is no easy job. But if we let him slip through the net now it would be no fun at all!'

'No, no, he'll come tonight, for sure . . . Hey, look! Look!' These last words, delivered in a whisper, took my breath away. A man in a black hat looked up at the gas lamp in front of Kado-ya, then vanished into the darkness. Not him. Uh-oh, I thought. Soon the clock downstairs struck ten, as loud as it pleased. It didn't look like this would be the big night after all.

A hush was settling over the whole neighborhood. We could hear the sound of a drum from the red-light district, so clear it made you feel like you could almost reach out and grab it. The moon stole up beyond the hills behind the hot spring, lighting up the street. And then, all of a sudden, we heard voices in the distance. Since we couldn't put our heads out the window, there was no way for us to see who it was, but they were evidently getting closer and closer. We could hear the clackety-clack of wooden sandals on the street. Peering at an angle through the peephole, we could finally make out two shadowy figures coming into view.

'Now that we've got him out of the way, everything will be all right.' There was no mistaking that voice: it was the Hanger-on.

'He was all bluster, no brainpower, so what could you expect?' This was Redshirt.

'That other one is a real Tokyo character. Still just a young-ster, but he does like to talk tough . . . Charming, isn't it!'

'Saying he doesn't want a raise, and trying to turn in his resignation . . . He must be mentally unbalanced, I'm sure of it.'

It was all I could do to keep myself from leaping straight down from the second floor and giving the two of them a good pounding right then and there. Laughing out loud, they walked through the light of the gas lamp and on into Kado-ya.

'Hey!'

'Hey!'

'There they are!'

'Finally!'

'What a relief!'

'Did you hear that? "Just a youngster, but he likes to talk tough" . . . Son of a bitch!!'

'But *I* was the one who was in the way – absolutely outrageous!'

The two of us would have to ambush them on their way home. But when would they be coming out? The Porcupine went downstairs to tell the man at the desk that he might have some business to attend to very late that night and to make sure that the door would be left open for us. Now that I think about it, we were pretty lucky that they let us out – for all they knew, we could have been burglars going to work!

Lying in wait for Redshirt to come along had been hard enough, but keeping our eyes peeled for the moment he came back out was even harder. We couldn't let ourselves doze off, and it was a pain keeping our faces pressed up against that opening in the window without a break; one way or another we couldn't help feeling on edge the whole time. I'd never had to do anything as hard in my entire life. I tried to convince the Porcupine that we might as well march right into Kado-ya and catch them red-handed, but this idea was rejected outright: if we barged in now, he said, we'd either be taken for a couple of hoodlums and stopped in our tracks, or, if we managed to explain why we were there and demanded to see Redshirt, they'd be sure to tell us he wasn't there or take us to the wrong room; and even if we somehow managed to get in without being noticed, we'd have no way of knowing which of the dozens of rooms to look for. There was nothing we could do but wait, boring as it was – and that's just what we did, all the way until five o'clock the next morning.

As soon as we saw the two of them coming out, the Porcupine and I set out after them. The first train back to the castle town wouldn't be leaving for a while yet, so they'd have to walk. From the edge of the hot spring village the road was lined with cedar trees for about a hundred yards, with rice paddies on either side. After that it ran along an embankment that passed through farmers' fields with some thatched houses here and there, and continued on up toward the castle grounds. Once we got out of the village we could overtake them anywhere we pleased. We decided that we'd try to catch them somewhere along the cedar avenue where there weren't any houses around, and shadowed them at a distance that allowed us to keep them in sight most of the time. As we passed the last of the village buildings we broke into a run, and came up behind them like a sudden windstorm. Dumbfounded, Redshirt turned around with no idea of what had hit him. We grabbed him by the shoulders and ordered them to halt. The Hanger was on the verge of panic and looked ready to make a run for it, so I wheeled around in front of him and cut off his line of escape.

'And just what was a man who occupies the position of Assistant Principal doing spending the night at Kado-ya?' demanded the Porcupine, wasting no time in getting the inquest under way.

'Am I to understand that some regulation prohibits Assistant Principals from spending the night there?' Redshirt's tone was as polished as ever, but his face looked slightly pale.

'And why did somebody who is so conscientious that he insists that even noodle shops and dumpling shops should be avoided on moral grounds see fit to spend a night at an inn in the company of a geisha?'

The Hanger was still on the lookout for an opportunity to run, so I stepped right in his way and yelled 'What do you mean, "just a youngster, but he likes to talk tough?"' right in his face.

'Oh, that wasn't you I was talking about, oh no, not at all . . .' Of all the shameless attempts to talk his way out of it! Just at that moment I noticed that my hands were still clutching tightly at my sleeves – when I came running up the road I had to grab them to keep the eggs I was carrying from knocking against each other. In a flash I stuck my hand in, pulled out two of them, and slammed them into the Hanger's face with a righteous yell. As they burst, the yolks began dripping down from the tip of his nose in a thick stream. Apparently shocked out of his wits, he flopped down onto his butt with a wail, then shouted 'Help! Help!!' Of course I had bought those eggs for eating, and I hadn't been keeping them in my sleeves to throw at anyone; in the heat of the moment, though, sheer rage had made me grab them and let the Hanger have it without even knowing what I was doing. But once I saw him sitting there miserably on his backside I realized that it had been just the right thing to do, so for good measure I pelted him with the rest of the eggs as well, screaming 'You goddamned son of a bitch!' as I let fly. His whole face was a mass of gooey yellow now.

While I was giving the Hanger the egg treatment, the Porcupine and Redshirt were keeping their wrangle going full blast:

'What proof do you have that I spent the night there with a geisha?'

'I saw your favorite geisha going into Kado-ya yesterday evening with my own eyes. If you think you can bluff your way out of this, forget it!'

'There's no need to bluff about anything. Yoshikawa and I stayed the night by ourselves. Whether a geisha went in there or not, it has nothing to do with us.'

'Just SHUT UP!' said the Porcupine, and socked him in the face. Redshirt took a few tottering steps, then mumbled 'This is unmitigated brutality! Blindly resorting to brute force, with no sense of right and wrong – it's inexcusable!'

'Don't you tell me what's inexcusable!' The Porcupine gave him another whack. 'This is the only way to make a snake like you understand!' he added for good measure, and went right on with the beating. While he was at it I kept myself busy pummeling the Hanger. Finally the two of them knelt cowering at the foot of a cedar; maybe they were too worn out to move, maybe it was just that their heads were swimming, but anyway they weren't even trying to escape.

'Had enough yet? If not, we'll give you some more,' the Porcupine shouted, and we began working them over again.

'Enough!'

I turned to the Hanger: 'And what about you? Had enough?'

'That's enough, of course!'

'This is the just punishment you rogues deserve. I hope you've learned your lesson and behave yourselves from now on. It doesn't matter how slick your excuses are – what's wrong is wrong, and you won't get away with it!' Neither of them made any reply to the Porcupine's warning. Probably by this point they just didn't feel up to saying anything.

'I'm not going to run and I'm not going to hide. If you want me for anything I'll be at Minato-ya down by the waterfront till five o'clock this evening. Go ahead and call in the police or anybody else if you want to.'

'I'm not running or hiding either,' I added. 'I'll be waiting with Hotta, so if you want to go to the police, go right ahead.' With that, the two of us strode off.

I got back to my place a little before seven and started packing right away. The old lady, of course, was surprised, and asked me what I was doing. 'I'm going to Tokyo, ma'am, to fetch my wife,' I told her, and, after settling the bill, I took the train down to the harbor and headed for Minato-ya. The Porcupine was in a second-floor room, asleep. I sat right down to write out a letter of resignation, but I didn't know what you were supposed to say so I simply wrote: 'Due to personal circumstances, I hereby resign. I am returning to Tokyo. Your understanding is appreciated.' Then I stuck it in an envelope, addressed it to the Principal, and mailed it off.

The boat was scheduled to sail at six that evening. Both of us, dead tired, fell into a deep sleep. By the time we woke up, it was two o'clock. We asked the maid if the police had been around, but apparently they hadn't. 'So Redshirt and the Hanger didn't lodge a complaint after all,' we said, and burst out laughing.

That evening the Porcupine and I left that accursed place behind us. The more distance the boat put between us and the shore, the happier we felt. From Kobe we took an express train straight to Tokyo. When we arrived at Shimbashi Station, I felt like I had finally made it out of purgatory and back to the real world. The Porcupine and I went our separate ways from there; I haven't had a chance to see him again since.

Oh, I almost forgot to say something about Kiyo. As soon as I set foot in Tokyo, I headed straight over to her place, suitcase and all, without even bothering to stop off at my old boarding-house. When I dashed through the doorway yelling 'Kiyo, I'm back!' she got all teary and said 'Botchan, oh my goodness! Back so soon!' I was so overwhelmed with relief that I announced right then and there that I would never go out to the country again and that I was going to get a house for both of us in Tokyo.

Not long afterward, through the good offices of an acquaintance of mine I got a job as an engineer on one of the streetcar lines. The salary was twenty-five yen a month, and my rent was six. Kiyo seemed perfectly satisfied with the house, even though it didn't have a fine entryway, but this February the poor woman caught pneumonia and died. The day before she died she called me to her bedside and said 'Botchan, for mercy's sake, please let me be buried at your family's temple when I die. I'll be happy just lying there, waiting for you to come.' And that's why her grave is in Yōgen Temple in Kobinata.

Penguin Classics

SANSHIRO
NATSUME SŌSEKI

'Even bigger than Japan is the inside of your head. Don't ever surrender yourself - not to Japan, not to anything'

Sōseki's work of gentle humour and doomed innocence depicts twenty-three-year-old Sanshiro, a recent graduate from a provincial college, as he begins university life in the big city of Tokyo. Baffled and excited by the traffic, the academics and - most of all - the women, Sanshiro must find his way amongst the sophisticates that fill his new life. An incisive social and cultural commentary, *Sanshiro* is also a subtle study of first love, tradition and modernization, and the idealism of youth against the cynicism of middle age.

In his introduction, Haruki Murakami reflects on his fascination with Sanshiro, how the story differs from a European coming-of-age novel and why it has come to be a perennial classic in Japan. This edition also contains suggestions for further reading, notes and a chronology.

Translated by Jay Rubin, with an introduction by Haruki Murakami

---

PENGUIN CLASSICS

THE MAN WHO WOULD BE KING: SELECTED STORIES
RUDYARD KIPLING

'They tell me that one never sees a dead person's face in a dream. Is that true?'

Rudyard Kipling is one of the most magical storytellers in the English language. This new selection brings together the best of his short writings, following the development of his work over fifty years. They take us from the harsh, cruel, vividly realized world of the 'Indian' stories that made his name, through the experimental modernism of his middle period to the highly-wrought subtleties of his later pieces. Including the tale of insanity and empire, 'The Man Who Would Be King', the high-spirited 'The Village that Voted the Earth Was Flat', the fable of childhood cruelty and revenge 'Baa Baa, Black Sheep', the menacing psychological study 'Mary Postgate' and the ambiguous portrayal of grief and mourning in 'The Gardener', here are stories of criminals, ghosts, femmes fatales, madness and murder.

Part of a series of new editions of Kipling's works in Penguin Classics, this volume contains a General Preface by Jan Montefiore and an introduction discussing Kipling's reputation and influence, the ambivalence of his writing and the fascination with 'otherness' expressed in his short works.

Edited with an introduction by Jan Montefiore
Series Editor Jan Montefiore

PENGUIN CLASSICS

THE RUBA'IYAT OF OMAR KHAYYAM

'Many like you come and many go
Snatch your share before you are snatched away'

Revered in eleventh-century Persia as an astronomer, mathematician and philosopher, Omar Khayyam is now known first and foremost for his *Ruba'iyat*. The short epigrammatic stanza form allowed poets of his day to express personal feelings, beliefs and doubts with wit and clarity, and Khayyam became one of its most accomplished masters with his touching meditations on the transience of human life and of the natural world. One of the supreme achievements of medieval literature, the reckless romanticism and the pragmatic fatalism in the face of death means these verses continue to hold the imagination of modern readers.

In this translation, Persian scholar Peter Avery and the poet John Heath-Stubbs have collaborated to recapture the sceptical, unorthodox spirit of the original by providing a near literal English version of the original verse. This edition also includes a map, appendices, bibliography and an introduction examining the *ruba'i* form and Khayyam's life and times.

'[Has] restored to that masterpiece all the fun, dash and vivacity' Jan Morris

Translated by Peter Avery and John Heath-Stubbs

THE STORY OF PENGUIN CLASSICS

Before 1946 ... 'Classics' are mainly the domain of academics and students; readable editions for everyone else are almost unheard of. This all changes when a little-known classicist, E. V. Rieu, presents Penguin founder Allen Lane with the translation of Homer's *Odyssey* that he has been working on in his spare time.

1946 Penguin Classics debuts with *The Odyssey*, which promptly sells three million copies. Suddenly, classics are no longer for the privileged few.

1950s Rieu, now series editor, turns to professional writers for the best modern, readable translations, including Dorothy L. Sayers's *Inferno* and Robert Graves's unexpurgated *Twelve Caesars*.

1960s The Classics are given the distinctive black covers that have remained a constant throughout the life of the series. Rieu retires in 1964, hailing the Penguin Classics list as 'the greatest educative force of the twentieth century.'

1970s A new generation of translators swells the Penguin Classics ranks, introducing readers of English to classics of world literature from more than twenty languages. The list grows to encompass more history, philosophy, science, religion and politics.

1980s The Penguin American Library launches with titles such as *Uncle Tom's Cabin*, and joins forces with Penguin Classics to provide the most comprehensive library of world literature available from any paperback publisher.

1990s The launch of Penguin Audiobooks brings the classics to a listening audience for the first time, and in 1999 the worldwide launch of the Penguin Classics website extends their reach to the global online community.

The 21st Century Penguin Classics are completely redesigned for the first time in nearly twenty years. This world-famous series now consists of more than 1300 titles, making the widest range of the best books ever written available to millions – and constantly redefining what makes a 'classic'.

The Odyssey continues ...

The best books ever written

PENGUIN ((^)) CLASSICS

SINCE 1946

Find out more at www.penguinclassics.com